# I AM GOD

## by G.R. McGill

# PROLOGUE

In the dwindling fog, he wipes the sweat off his forehead. He is happy. He looks down at the lifeless and sunken face of his once closest ally. This so called friend had betrayed him and deserved nothing but death. He had tried to bring shame on his sister and that, he could never forgive. He wouldn't have anyone bring shame to his family and surely not under his name would a bastard be born in his family.

He had dug the hole deep enough and now he started to refill it. He began to lay the stones of the foundations for his house on top of the body.

They had talked together about how this spot was a good place to start a new hamlet – the village they had grown up in across the water from here was now nothing. Ruined by ruffians, and as friends they had spent a long time building a small huddle of the good families, including the vicar. These were the people of morals and beliefs, who feared God – these were the true people of God, who were not scared to start a fresh and sin free life.

He didn't have time to dwell on his loss, he was already thinking of his new haven, and how he had chosen a great spot, a great name:Valhan. He knew it was going to be a long journey, but he would rather sleep at peace with an ache in his bones, than lay in a dwelling amongst lawless louts.

The vicar had already set the motions by applying for a new Parish so that his people wouldn't have to travel too far. From what they had heard in the last correspondence, it looked like it would go ahead. He would tell everyone that his friend had run away. He would convince them that it was only him left now

– the true leader of their community – and he was sure once everyone saw the haven he had chosen, they would follow him. He was sure of that. He had promised his sister to the Vicar so that would secure his standing in this new world.

For now he thinks less of the problems and more of the success of this new settlement. He would ensure that his whole family came here and would never associate with the ruffians of their home village ever again. He would ensure that his family name would be the driving force of Valhan. He would build the most respectable community ever, and not a single bastard could ever set foot in his pure little world.

# CHAPTER ONE

You may not believe me, but it's true. I can see everything. I know what lies in your heart and mind. I know you better than you know yourself.

Yes, even you, curled up so innocently on your sofa with a book in your lap, or you, whilst you pretend to be engrossed in your work but are busy picking the last bacterial nasal mucus that clings so tenaciously to your nose lining. Then, there is you – you are pretending to browse important stuff, but I can see what you are typing, I can see the truth in your eyes as they light up with dark desire, I can see you look over your shoulder in case your family member walks in and catches you looking at the images, the gifs and the videos.

I don't get any pleasure from watching you. Don't be fooled for one minute. I, unlike you, don't watch other humans from my screens for pleasure. Human beings make me sick and I am so glad that I am above all your sickness, desires and weakness.

I know you still don't believe me. This is you just being a silly human and not understanding my true importance. I know you think I am insane and once again you are utterly wrong. If you wish to open your eyes and understand who I am, I suggest that you come on a journey. On a journey that will show you that I Am God and I know everything about you.

Power: is a funny thing isn't it? Power only empowers those who truly deserve it, those who can handle it, and I can tell you that when power came hunting for me, I stood tall like a true warrior and thrived in the challenge of the attack. I am not one of those weaklings who sees power and runs from it. I stand here and embrace it and allow it to enrich my every living cell. We are in a true equilibrium, power and I.

At the start of this journey, I did feel a bit doomed, but I was always looking for my chance to escape from my so called life and so I worked hard and diligently at the start. That chance, my first job as an IT tech, was my escape from that wretched wicked witch who you shall get to know soon enough. It was offered to me after a stint of unpaid work experience via the school. The manager had liked my attitude toward work and my quick understanding of her company's software systems, so she offered me a part time job.

I was doing the usual online discussions; you know the one where you give me permission to access your computer and I can then fix any problems.

The mind-numbing calls I had to endure. Oh, believe me the stereotypes are true you know!

"Sir, have you switched your machine on?"

"Is it plugged in?"

I seriously could have strangled some of you for your sheer levels of stupidity. How can you seriously be so utterly dim witted as not to switch your machine on?

Oh, please don't roll your eyes; it's true there are people who are that clueless living on this planet right now, breathing the same air as I do. The same kind of despicable people whom on hearing my voice questioned my knowledge of IT. Those same idiots questioned my age and credibility. It enraged me when the user on the end acted superior because they had learnt a few tech words. How they would throw them into the conversation to try and pretend to me that they knew what they were talking about. Seriously! If I could, I would insert a roll-eye emoji right here. Spare me the ignorance – I am not the one who is calling for help so don't you dare underestimate my ability.

At this point, I have to thank you, the stupid people of this world. It was one boring, sunny morning, whilst on a mid-term break from school, sitting in the dungeon of some building that looked far more glamorous from the outside than the inside, that I realised the power I could have over you.

I was chatting to a hapless user who had given me complete control of his PC. He had toddled off to make a cup of tea because he was, "Fed up and stressed with the Monday morning drama of his computer not working." It had not taken me long – 60 seconds actually – to fix the user's "stupid computer doesn't work" issue. Mr self-proclaimed "normally really good at IT stuff" had managed to freeze his company's cheap mass-produced laptop by downloading too many large files at once. Whilst he was away, I started to meddle with the programming and discovered that a simple change to the settings on his computer would  keep me logged onto his software and hardware.

When misery guts came back with his cup of tea, he saw a lovely little pop-up note that informed him that I had now logged out of his device. Instead I was there, looking at him from my screen, watching him peering at the note, and then rolling his eyes and tapping furiously at his keyboard, before he realised that I had actually fixed his "unfixable issue on his stupid device".

I stayed logged on for as long as I could without getting caught. At this point my mind was going crazy. I wanted to yell in excitement. As I sat there with misery guts' computer running in the background, my mind whirred with the possibilities of what this meant for me.

So my journey had started from there. I slowly applied a few changes to misery guts' computer which meant that I would remain logged in all the time. The trouble I had at this stage was I didn't have a computer at home as my Nana wouldn't allow "this new-fangled disease" into our house. So the only changes and work I could do was either at my job, the library or school.

Even from there, with basic tools, little knowledge, and lack of access, I managed to change a few details here and there on his computer. I guess the empowering part was when I managed to then log onto his personal computers. At that point my own knowledge was weak, but there was one thing that I had learnt, and that is you my little minions don't actually know much, especially when it comes to your computers, smart phones and smart TVs.

Knowledge is power. I, at that point in my life, had a huge thirst for it, and as my knowledge increased so did my gap from you humans.

It was very amusing for me at the start; I picked a few of you as my experiments. I would laugh with glee watching the expressions on your face as I started switching your computer on and off, or made your phone suddenly freeze or slow down whilst you were in the middle of a heated discussion on twitter about politics (which, let's face it you know nothing about, though the reduced character count allows you to spew some nonsense and pretend you are eloquent). I loved switching your TV off at a crucial scene. To annoy some of you cretins, I would switch the TV on in the middle of you going to bed or log on randomly to your accounts on your TV whilst you were watching. For those of you who have a smart TV, when you suddenly see that sign that says "logging into your email account" – that's usually my software doing that.

What started off as mild voyeurism led me to manage, manipulate and conjure up a few codes that resulted in my very first app being developed.

From there it was easy to create apps for every type of human being. Teenagers, fashionistas, sporty types and the gamers.

My first, and to date most successful, app was aimed at your darling little children.

It's a free app. My main aim wasn't to make money through it. I just needed a means to get into your software. The money it generated through the free advertisements was useful, especially as my Nana never gave me any money. She much preferred it to be gathering dust in the vaults of the banks, rather than give it to me.

If you know the right websites, the right streams, the right people and have access to the right technology it is then very easy to manipulate marketing and numbers. A few favours from some online friends meant that my app was constantly thrown into social media sites. A few changes to numbers and the "downloaded 100 times" was changed to 1000 or 10,000 times. See, the way to get away with this type of manipulation is to do it subtly so that the main host support team doesn't get alerted. It's like running a stealth operation. I created fake profiles, fake companies and slowly marketed the app and its reviews until it naturally became a huge hit. One of my top marketing successes was making a cute You-Tube video that was shared on every mummy, daddy or carer's Facebook pages, and then creating the anti-cute video where the bear says some rude stuff. Share that on a few student pages and trending hashtags, and suddenly everyone is talking about it. The teddy is made into gifs, sent as messages, Snaps, Instas and retweeted – before you know it, a seemingly silly app has become one of the most downloaded apps in the last five years.

It really is a clever little app, my little creation: a true reflection of my genius. So of course I have to tell you more as I am sure you would love to download it. Also I doubt that you will understand what it is unless I explain it you.

My app is called: My First Teddy.

The whole purpose is to build your bespoke teddy bear. You get to design its fur. You are lucky – for a free app, you get so many colours and skins to choose from. Things like the sharpness factor of the bear's claws are in your control, and it also has a cuddle factor!

You can record mummy and daddy's voice and give it to the bear. So whilst you the ever so busy parent is doing everything but comforting and playing with your child, you can hand them the technology and a little cartoon will talk to your child in your voice via my app. A little app and a friendly little bear can keep your child engrossed for quite a while.

In my second upgraded version of this app I also let you superimpose your child's or friend's face onto another teddy bear to be teddy's friend. You can then create a little cartoon snap. Or a video of your little one playing with his creative teddy bear.

I just needed access, let's be honest. The appeal to send videos to your ever-suffering family and friends is never ending. You send them a short video of your child in a cartoon playing with a teddy that they designed. The video carries spyware, so once they download it, I have access to and control of their software. The amount of students that sent this video when I made an adult version of drunk teddy was beyond even my imagination.

I didn't want to lose the parents, so I created more for them: Christmas videos, postcards, anything you want and all free, no in-app purchases, no different levels, no one-off payments. Everything on My First Teddy app is free.

Of course you could have caught me out. All you had to was read my overly complicated, cleverly drafted terms and conditions, put on exactly forty four pages of tiny print: font level six.

If you were tenacious enough to read them you would then need a PHD in English literature to decipher that one silly sentence which states that you have now agreed to the additional functionality designed to monitor and spy on you. I wanted someone to catch me out, prove to me that you were as good as I was, but it never did happen. You all just click agree so quickly without even reading the first sentence.

So now I see the bemused look of incredulous disbelief. So I have control; so what? Oh my dear children of the world, let me show you exactly what I am capable of.

I warn you now this is not for the faint hearted and there may be some flash backs, those that come to haunt me. I am glad they do. They keep me focused and stop me turning into a monster like you humans.

# CHAPTER TWO

I never had a real need for money. You see, my clever mind enjoyed the control and as I speak to you now, here I am sitting in front of my mothership, the epicentre of my genius.

I sit in front of my screens and watch you all. I've coded you into categories. You humans are funny like that – you want to be different, to be noticed, to stand out from the crowd and yet you seem to thrive best when you blend in.

It wasn't hard to categorise you at all. Surprisingly, I found myself enjoying the task of putting you all into boxes and then watching how you all lived up to the stereotype I had chosen for you.

So follow me as I take you into the category of the overbearing "I love my kid more than myself" parent. You know the ones – they spend their entire life marketing to the world, usually on Facebook or Instagram, just how special their kid is. Perhaps that's you. Well you see I have captured the life of your children for my own investment and now I have your pictures of your little children to sell to various users.

I need some of these other users to help me, so for now I tolerate them. Technology, rules and updates change constantly in my world, and sometimes I just need a reminder or some backup in case I missed something. Although that is not going to happen. I do not take the risk. These changes don't normally slip past my radar, but I always have a backup. And a little give and take from one screen user allows me to keep updated and not get caught. A particularly clever screen user who is smart enough to understand the changes around the spyware detection techniques used, well he passes me the relevant information which then in turn allows me to update and change my T&Cs. A little exchange of these types of favours allows us to exist without clashes. Although my friend doesn't know that I know who he is and I watch him constantly. The day he becomes useless or annoying to me, I can easily destroy his existence. This particular user, who is one of the nicer ones that I chat to, thinks I need the updates so that I can keep my job. It pays to act helpless, vulnerable and the right gender to the right people.

I suggest you get yourself a cup of tea and enjoy the story as it unfolds.

Let me start your journey here, with a lovely lady called Clara Hall. I have to thank you, Clara, for the constant pictures and videos of your child. You were my perfect target when I first started: one of the many bored stay-at-home mums.

The good thing about the Claras of this world is that they never put their phones down. So I would sit and wait, not long mind you, and here we go click, click click – post on Facebook. "Little Charlie looking cute even though he has done a stinky poo." She uploads a pic of an average-looking Charlie.

I am sending Clara a targeted marketing message, something I know that will peak her interest, because I know what she has been looking at and I know what makes her tick.

Bingo! The new update on her favourite baby clothes pings. The notification pops up and suddenly her overtly motherly devotion is lost to the draw of the world wide web. Little Charlie is lying there forgotten whilst mummy is too busy tapping into her screen and pointing the phone at him for pictures. He rarely has eye to eye contact with his mum. He was, it seems, born looking at his parents via a camera. His mum is now someone who is far more interested in the number of likes she has received, simultaneously checking baby clothes online, whilst she absentmindedly stands next to Charlie in case he rolls off the changing table.

My mastermind station has already hacked into her phone, television, the baby monitor – anything with a camera and sound recording – and I suddenly have savoury and not so savoury footage of her little darling Charlie. Clara downloaded My First Teddy even before her Charlie was born. She is a keen social media mum but she is also lonely and uses the technology for communication, to show the world how busy her lonely existence is.

Whilst Clara was so busy tapping away, furiously replying to people who are liking her Facebook update and trying to bookmark baby clothes all at the same time, I was getting close ups of Charlie, his room, his changing station and his life.

Little Charlie's progress updates are being sold to a couple in some part of Asia that wanted to raise an Internet baby. They in turn keep my online currency at a very healthy balance. When I started, I had to do a lot of the AI work manually. Now I have a constant stream. Dearest Clara, you and your family are on your very own Big Brother show. You just do not know it.

Now you can't really judge me or hate me. You see, I am not the one constantly on my smartphone, or sitting in front of the TV, or on my pads, pods, laptops and voice control devices. I am just streaming to the world what you are giving me access to. Thanks to new technology that allows you to play music when you want, and switch your lights on and off by just using voice command, I now know what you are up to when your camera based technology is all switched off.

When I started, I was naïve, but also a nobody in this world of the dark net. To raise my profile and establish my power, I had to sell my material to a lot of people who are worse than the shit that comes out of a buffoon with Diarrhoea. These humans who have no morals or any tendency to display any signs of humanity, they only wish to fulfil their deepest and darkest desires and well, if I must be honest, whilst on the path to supremacy, I was happy to trade with these people and take their money. I will let your imagination take you down the murky road I had to endure and why people like me rule the dark net.

#

For as long as I can remember I was verbally, physically and mentally abused by the witch who shall be referred to as Nana, My Grandmother.

Nana was an old-fashioned woman, who really should have been alive in pre-historic times. She was a tall lady and many times as a child I heard murmuring of how she had not aged well. Once, she was the beauty of our little town, Valhan, but her life had been hard on her and any superficial beauty had faded. As my numbness grew, my feelings for her diminished. Originally, I had tried to please her to get some warmth from her, but when a plant is not nourished it wilts and dies, and in its place a weed will grow. Now weeds do get given a bad reputation, but they are resistant. After years of adaptation they can survive a heatwave, a storm and eventually if not taken care of properly they will take over everything. Unlike your precious flowers that you love and nurture daily: they will wilt at the first sign of adversity. The weed will survive, and this was something that I knew how to do very well.

Nana hated me from the day she was told by her precious daughter that I was going to be born. She hated me for my "wicked father", who had clearly tricked her precious little girl and made her pregnant. Her daughter was stupid enough to believe that if she kept me, then the man who had run away at the mere news of the unplanned pregnancy would return.

He never did, and my Mother died from a broken heart – I was to later find out it was suicide, but my twisted Nana couldn't face reality and had spun the story into some tragic fairy tale.

I never knew any other family. Nana was my carer, and ironically there was no care involved.

I grew up in our ancestral home, one of the few original buildings left standing in the town. Valhan is an old-style town where everyone knows everyone, and people still believe in marriages, and have many Victorian type houses and similar ideologies.

The good times with Nana were when we sat down in front

of the open fire together and we both had our cup of tea – a true source of therapy for anyone. Nana told me stories of "her" ancestors and how they had been in this part of the world since records had begun, from helping to build the local church with their bare hands, to being the village doctor. She told me of how she was lucky to have married her dream man, who had supported her decision never to leave this rickety old town or her ancestral home. She would smile often when she told me the story of her pregnancy news and how happy they had been.

Then her face would become twisted as she remembered her precious child and how I was the reason she had died. Then the abuse would begin.

"You are the bastard who has ruined my family name." She would stand tall in front of me, kicking and punching when the anger and frustrations became too much for her. "My ancestors will be turning in their graves knowing that a bastard has been born into this family. Your father is responsible for the ruin of this family!

"They came here to start a life away from crime. Crime created by bastard people like you – they laid the very first stones in this town."

I learned those lines. I heard them before she could even deliver them.

The beatings were carefully planted around my body so that they wouldn't see the marks at school. Her favourite and go-to physical act of violence was pulling my hair, so hard at times it came out, and if I cried she would continuously slap me till I stopped crying. Now I know we are living in the 21st century but my Nana's family clearly were a backward family. One who had held their heads high with some fake pride over social etiquette and place in society. It wasn't until I was at school that I learnt that most children now are born out of wedlock and being a bastard isn't the sin that I was led to believe. Nearly fifty percent of the population in this country are born out of wedlock. Once upon a time to have been born out of wedlock would have been the biggest embarrassment and the biggest curse that you could place on your family, but now it has become a common thing.

Yet I was punished daily. I stopped crying a long time ago. The only thing I started focusing on was washing every piece of my body that she had touched. I mentally started to map it out on my body, and when she stopped I would calmly pick myself up and scrub off her germs. After my rigorous shower or bath, I would come down and make myself some tea, and breathe.

She initially watched me carry out my ritual with disbelief. Sometimes she would stand there watching me, shaking her head. I was too young to understand what she was thinking. I would always ignore her, but eventually she would wander off to look after her cherished garden that was abundant with flowers and shrubs – she particularly liked the old stones at the side of the wall that were apparently the first stones laid down by our ancestor, the founder of Valhan – or she would sulk off to the study to read up on the local newsletters and journals for local events. She loved her family's or even her own presence in the town, and how ther ancestors never moved from the very first house that was ever built. The council had tried to see if they could make the stones a tourist point, but our family had refused as they firmly believed a curse would befall them if the stones were moved or touched.

I tried to escape the abuse at home, and from the local kids for being dressed like an orphan child, another deliberate abuse, delivered so easily by Nana. She would tell me, "No point making you look all modern. It will only attract the wrong type of attention. School is for studying, not a place to make friends." So I made friends with the other misfits, which she was not happy with.

The intelligent children, the children from different backgrounds, they welcomed someone like me. I was clever and due to my Nana's connections within the community I was still given preferential treatment by the authorities in the school.

Although studying began as my way to hide in the library or stay confined in my room without being confronted by

Nana, I soon started to realise the importance of education, computers, technology, and how I could use them as an escape mechanism. This is where I learnt that I was actually good at something. Modern technology was far too advanced for Nana to understand, so she couldn't destroy my faith in it. To escape from her, I also took as much work as I could over the school holidays. She had to allow me to go as I had manipulated the headmaster into writing me a letter of referral and about the importance of doing pre-university work. Nana wouldn't have wanted to say no to the headmaster of the only school in town and run the risk of becoming someone who people talked about for the wrong reasons.

Nana and her family were old Valhanians – the residents of Valhan Town. As a child I accompanied Nana to many social events. Nana was very well known and respected. People came to our house to ask for her advice and Nana, to the outside world, was a very strong and respected lady. A lady who had survived losing her husband, raised her daughter in difficult times and then went on to survive the loss of her only child. I was sometimes smiled at, but mostly everyone who visited us was too scared of Nana to mention me, or ask about me without her mentioning me first.

I was just the quiet little child who sat there un-noticed, unassuming yet quietly observing everything. It was a good thing, because it taught me a lot about human nature, how easily people can change their opinions, and be openly fake not only to the person in front of them, but to themselves, just to ensure they were seen to be part of the crowd.

Nana had one particularly good friend out of all her cronies: Celia Burton. Celia had been Nana's friend since time began – well it felt like that to me as a child. Nana seemed to tell her everything, and also when all the parties would finish, Celia would stay over for a cup of tea, a biscuit, and the real gossip. I would spend many an afternoon listening to them talking of how they could right the wrongs of Valhan and the world.

Celia was also the only one who was brave enough to ever

come over and talk to me and ask me how I was. Although a smaller, and far quieter and shyer woman than Nana, Celia was not afraid of Nana. She was a busy body, and knew everything, and for Nana she served a good purpose as a confidant and someone to reminisce with.

Celia's daughter Shone had also been friends with my mum, Abi, at school. Before Shone had married and started her own life, she used to come over, and every time she saw me, she would burst into tears, hug me, and try and hold me close. I hated her visits. They usually meant that when she left, Nana would get upset with the memories, and that would lead to some form of beating or mental torture. With time I learnt that whenever Shone and Celia came, I should make sure I was well out of sight. It is a survival of the fittest and smartest thing.

# CHAPTER THREE

At age 16, most people were out there getting laid and drunk. I had already been accepted for a degree in computer science showing exceptional aptitude in the subject, but this news made my Nana angry. She, of course, was outraged that I had even entertained the thought of leaving her. She had angrily thrown some of her precious family heirlooms to the ground. Luckily for her own sanity and my safety none of them had broken. She then got angrier and angrier. I remember this clearly because she did not hit me straight away like I had imagined she would. She paced up and down, slamming things and shouting louder and louder, then she came storming toward me like a twister, and I had tried not to flinch as she told me she would not fund me, nor would she welcome me back if I left.

"I will leave the money to cats and dogs rather than leave it to a bastard like you!" she said, as flecks of spit hit my face. "You are showing your true bastard blood and running away like your father."

That was a crucial moment for me, for then I just knew what to do. It was one of those pivotal moment in life when the path is clear and you know what needs to be done. Have you ever experienced that? You just know what you have to do and everything else just doesn't matter anymore. I was no longer small enough for her to physically hurt me anymore and she too was becoming frail. Her words, however, had a way of ripping off that cover I had created, and spooning out my gut like a hungry man would the inside of a water melon.

For a while, as she started to rant, I just watched in slow and probably silent motion. What brought me back to reality was when I saw the confusion in her old face, her eyes narrowing at me trying to understand why a blank expression had replaced the old resigned one.

"I will cut you off – don't doubt it!" she growled and I just stood there: I stood there taller, stronger, more able and probably more willing to inflict more damage than she had ever been capable of.

Nana had hurt me out of an emotional rage. I could hurt with no emotions attached.

From that day onwards I was the puppet master. I had full control over the estate, monies and Nana.

I knew then that leaving Nana alone now was a liability as she was scared, and I could not trust her actions if she did decide to go off on an emotionally fuelled rampage. So I put in a special request, based around the fact that I was the sole carer for my Nana and I could not attend University physically, but could learn online. I was granted my special request and I was able to do my degree remotely via Zoom or skype, online tutorials, and only a few days a month where I needed to check in or go sit exams with a local hub that was affiliated with the main University.

From that day Nana stopped hitting me – she was scared, I could sense it, so she threw herself into her gardening and social events, leaving me alone. I completed my four year degree in a record three-years – first class of course. We attended the ceremony, and we both kept our distance from the proud and happy families. Nana came along only for show. She couldn't have had the people of Valhan talk about how she had neglected my graduation day. We only had one photograph taken, and only because Nana needed something to show her friends to help keep up appearances.

From that day my plan to exclude Nana from any social gatherings began. Nana had a strong social network surrounding her, so I had to think very carefully of how to dismantle it, and how to slowly wean her away.

The one thing I had at my disposal were Nana's emotions. As

a child I had learnt very quickly when she was going to start to lose her cool, and it didn't take much, so I tried avoiding doing all those things that would enrage her, but now I could use this knowledge to my advantage.

I went from being a quiet and obedient child in public, to a quiet and slightly mischievous adult. Like the time I openly started to flirt with one of Nana's friends right in front of Nana, and it was only Nana who could see what I was doing. She was so used to keeping her cool in public and only losing it in private, that when her rage kicked in she started yelling in the community hall in front of everyone – one long bellow echoed through the small walls of the hall. I, like the superhero grandchild that I am, I went to help.

Nana was embarrassed by her outburst and stood in silence, her mouth now closed but twisted in rage. I went to her and she started to slap me away in front of everyone. I loved how my plans worked so well. This time she realised everyone could see, so she had feigned weakness and leant into me. I had never realised that she was such a good actress. I took her into the side room and came back out quickly to take her some tea. Whilst making the tea, I started to tell the local busybodies that had swarmed me about how her mental state was poor, and there were very clear signs of dementia and anxiety showing – and that this, of course, was the main reason I had not gone off to university and left her all alone.

They all started to nod and shake their heads almost simultaneously, like it was some form of ritual.

I slowly started to attend the many functions alone, till the invites stopped coming for Nana. I took every opportunity I could to worsen the image of Nana's deteriorating health. I am proud to admit that I never inflicted any physical pain on her to comply, and had just an emotional torture routine. In her last few outings, I simply and slowly raised my hand the way I always did before I hurt her with my taunts, and she started to tremble and cry uncontrollably. Her friends, instead of helping her, had looked on helplessly whilst once again I, the true hero, stepped forward to help my Nana. The problem -still -with having mental health issues, is that in some communities people fear you, and think if they come too close you may attack them.

For my plan to fully come to fruition I had to wait till our local doctor went on holiday, then I hacked into our local GP system, where I changed Nana's prescription and changed her medical notes. There was a little subtle note and ticks against early signs of dementia. I changed her medicine strength and processed it all within minutes.

I then had to wait for my Nana's quarterly tea party that she hosted for all her friends. I gave her a tablet for her type two diabetes, but the stronger one, the one that would make her sugar lower than normal. She had been diagnosed with this type of diabetes, which occurred due to stress, and mostly she controlled it well. She was fit for her age and didn't eat bad foods. Her sugars were good, but a stronger tablet would make her hypoglycaemic. I needed her to have a low sugar episode in front of her friends. A low sugar episode manifests itself in different ways for different people, and for Nana, it made her weak and angry. She would have a fear of death, and she would feel faint and dizzy. I had seen her experience this once, and had found it surprisingly frightening, but now that I knew how to deal with it, I wanted her friends to experience it so that they would stop coming.

Like always, Nana had been busy running about preparing for the event, bossing the caterers to no end, and just being her bullish old self. Deep down she knew I had a hand in why she wasn't openly invited to events, and this was her chance to prove to her fellow Valhanians that there was nothing wrong with her! Finally, when she had the chance to stop, she took her double strength tablet on an empty stomach. She did reach out to quickly eat something, but was distracted by the caterer, so her body responded to the medicine at exactly the same time as her friends parked their bottoms on her lovely couch. She started to sweat. I stood in the background, like always, watching and waiting for the effects of the low sugar to kick in.

She started to mumble incoherently. Her friends started to ask if she was OK, but she was getting frustrated, and started to push them away, giving poor old Mary a good hard thwack across the hand, whilst still mumbling and sweating. They looked worried. I took my time to step forward, then sighed and looked as worried as I could for my Nana whilst I escorted her out to the kitchen. There, I gave her a strong sugary drink, whilst shoving a glucagon tablet in her mouth. I left her sitting, shaking on the cold tiles of the kitchen floor.

I then made myself as remorseful as I could, and took myself back to the sitting room. Shaking my head and wearing a slight pout, I said slowly and lightly, "I just don't think Nana can host these any more. I'm sorry you had to see her have an attack – even if it was a mild one."

Her friends looked horrified, and keenly took in my stories of Nana's outbursts – of how she would forget who she was, how she would lash out, and how I was scared sometimes when we were alone, but I would manage because I would never put her in a home. They all looked at me admiringly, but that was the last time any of them ever ventured into our house. Since that incident they would, in a well-meaning manner, of course, enquire nicely about Nana whenever they saw me. Celia had tried to stay back at the tea party that day and almost put my plan into jeopardy, but thankfully I managed to usher her out with the promise that I would keep her up to date by calling her to arrange for her to come over. Celia was the only one who ever came back: the rest of Nana's so-called friends scuttled off as fast as they could.

By that time I was old enough to inherit, so there was no need for Nana and to be honest, there was no enjoyment in my hurting her. I never hit her, but emotionally and mentally I made her realise how much damage I could do. My wounds had been imbedded too deeply to be soothed by causing her any physical harm. I had a lot more fun taunting her, ignoring her and then making her believe I was going to hurt her.

For example, I did rather enjoy discussing the arrangements

for her cremation whilst she was alive, and watching the horror grow in her eyes as she realised I would never allow her to be buried in her family plot. Watching her face sadden when it dawned on her she would not be laid to rest next to her beloved husband, or her precious daughter. I had told her rather pointedly one day, "Well let's face it Nana, I have to ensure that you rest in peace – I can't have you tossing and turning in your grave like the rest of your ancestors." The look she gave me was one of pure hatred and sadness mixed together, and I was immune to it. She bloody well made me into this monster – she could live with the consequences of it for a short while longer.

Here is another thing that surprised me: how long a human being that old can last under the weight of a cushion on their face.

The old witch had attempted to try and grab my head, to grab some hair, and when she couldn't reach she had tried to slap at my arms and my face. Her valiant efforts lost to my sheer will power. I had left her still breathing, but I knew her last breath would be of her own choice. I went into my haven – my room in the attic and lay there listening to Beethoven's "Fur Elise". I then went for my morning jog, slightly earlier than normal, and when I came back you can only imagine my distraught and anguish at losing my only relative – my cleaner Martha had discovered her whilst I was out.

I am not sure where the tears came from, but they did come, and in the kitchen I nearly spilt boiling water from the kettle on my hand. Martha had to take over and make me some tea. She said some sympathetic words, but I didn't hear them. I just sat there and drank my tea, for once not rushing to the shower room. I had made sure the doctor who would come was able to sign the certificate and put down old age as a cause of death.

I attended her cremation service after much consideration – I kept my head down, and Celia had been the only one who had offered to give a speech. Her speech described a different Nana, the carefree girl who had loved Valhan more than anything. She told everyone of how Nana and she had fallen in love with the same boy, Thomas, but Celia had seen how he looked at Nana and had gallantly stepped aside to let true love flourish. She spoke of Nana as a sister rather than a friend. I listened to the stories, of how Nana and my Grandfather were like the golden couple, and how everyone had wanted a wedding like theirs. I looked around and everyone was crying or nodding with nostalgic faces. Celia went on to talk of how Nana had wanted a wedding to knock New York off its posts, and everyone laughed. It would seem Nana's wedding had been quite the event, but this was not my memory of the shell that lay in that box.

Eventually Celia had spoken of her heartbreak, from the day Thomas had died tragically, then Abigail, then to the day Nana had started to lose her mind, and how she was glad that finally Nana was at peace with the people she loved most. She spoke of me, the honourable grandchild who had done more than anyone could ask for. I held my tissue to my nose and shook my head, muttering how I hadn't done enough. Whilst those who sat next to me patted my back, all I could think of was *god I need to burn these clothes!*

Martha, my cleaner, helped sort the day out, and helped tidy up the mess of the wake. Although I had no time to think of the mulling and shaking of heads, I did not want to take the risk of not attending the cremation and the wake. Martha had been excellent in keeping me informed on what the locals were saying and doing when Nana's death had been announced. The local hall had run it's customary tea and consolation service to help all those who needed it. In the front row at the service sat all of Nana's so-called friends, those very ones who were only faithful to her when she was well. As soon as they thought she wasn't well enough, not one of them had bothered to even call in – the only one had been Celia – a true loyal heart.

None of these things matter to me. I know how fickle and selfish you human beings are – which is why I keep my distance. I don't know why, but just this moment a very strong but vivid memory came back into my mind and it was the day Nana called me an evil soul!

Nana was wrong that day you know: she had told me I was "an evil soul". This was on the day of the Robin's eggs.

Let's be honest, if there is nothing inside you, it can't be evil or good. It's just a huge vat of nothingness.

Now my followers, this day indeed was an important one, as it made me realise that when you don't have good or evil inside of you, then you decide what you want to be, and on this particular day I established my need for power. Let me tell you the full story as I am sure you must desperate to hear it.

By chance one day, in the farthest corner of the massive gardens of our house, I sat and watched the Robins. I was intrigued by them and I came back to the same spot the day after and noticed the patterns from across the bench. I kept my distance. I had read up about them after first spotting them and had learnt about their habits – these little birds were easily spooked.

I watched them communicate and could almost hear them agreeing on their chosen spot that they would call home.

The garden to the house begins with the usual patio area. There is a small mini wall, which was kept open with a path running through the middle. The path covers an acre of the vast garden and is made with symmetrical hexagon shaped stones with mosaic tiles on the edges. The path takes you across to the garden with ornaments on both sides flowing with different coloured flowers, ornaments that had taken generations to amass and create this floral museum. Nana had always loved gardening but she was growing old at this stage so she had hired help. Of course hired help also made Nana think she was very important.

Our gardens always looked immaculate and right at the back of the path there were a few stairs that led up to a small wooden gazebo. I love this place; it empowers me. The gazebo was built by hand by one of our family – a garden wedding for one of the more cherished non-bastard offspring. And it was here that I sat and watched the Robins agree that a small hole at the side of one of the show piece ornaments would be the place to start building a home.

I had watched for weeks, the adult female bird collecting the moss and the leaves to make their nests, I had watched her build it, I prepared for the days she would lay her eggs. Robins lay one egg a day like most birds, but to complete their clutch they usually lay up to four eggs. From a distance I watched her incubating the eggs and only leaving them for a sparse few minutes to go and eat.

I was obsessed until the incubation period. At first it had intrigued me the way the eggs were rotated and how nurturing the birds actually were to their eggs, but a few days into the incubation period I became bored and angry. I walked over to the nest and threw stones at the birds. I watched them flap away from the barrage of missiles.

I walked over to the nest and looked curiously at the eggs. I picked them up one by one and held all 4 warm eggs in my hands, the whole unborn family in my hands. I looked up and in the distance I saw Nana standing on the patio, squinting her eyes whilst trying to watch me. I walked slowly but purposefully over towards her, turning the eggs in my hand slowly, their warmth unsettling me slightly, but not enough to stop me.

As I reached the patio area, I looked into her eyes and one at a time I picked up the eggs and held them eye level high. I dropped them one at a time and watched her face as she witnessed them smash onto the hard tiles of the patio. I didn't blink, but she flinched, gasped and shuddered at the same time, and that my friends was the first time ever I had seen fear in her eyes. That was the day I felt I had the right to be powerful. That was the day I felt something that you normal people might describe as happiness.

# CHAPTER FOUR

Back to the present day. I am finally alone in "her ancestral home", a beautiful property with a grand hallway that is bigger than most people's houses, and a staircase that goes up from both sides, joined at the top by a wide corridor that leads off to the five grand bedrooms. You can stand in the middle of the corridor and lean on the mahogany balcony – carefully constructed by one of the few craftsmen that had lived in Valhan, of course – and look down into the hallway.

Underneath the left staircase is my study, once formally the guest sitting room, and under the right staircase is a lounge split into two spaces. On the left of the room is the formal seating area and on the right is a dining room that leads into the kitchen. The kitchen and laundry room are the bones of the original building, and over the years they have been built on and adapted. A couple of years ago, I had all the old decor changed, much to Nana's disgust. Much to my disgust, she wouldn't let me decorate her room. When my mum passed away, Nana had moved in. I agreed to her persistence, and her show of defiance had actually amused me. I had everything plastered down and painted white; the freshness of white paint refreshed me beyond anything. I also had all the old flowery and musty carpets replaced by clean wooden floor. She, of course, had hated that I'd got rid of her formal entertaining space.

It truly is a house meant for a grandiose family, for the sound of human noise, children laughing, dogs barking, cats lurking around corners and the smell of homemade bread.

A house that had once been filled with human warmth is now

just a place for me to stay whilst I control the world. The only movement you can hear is the electric buzz of my machines, the pinging, and the faint music I play in the background, through my built-in speakers.

The music, of course, has to be classical.

When I was younger, I found refuge in our attic. I call this place my haven. I loved hiding up there – unlike the attics of other houses, it wasn't full of junk, and as time went on and I started to claim my dominance, this was the first place that I made my own. Not even Nana could glimpse into it. The reason it had become my haven first was that Nana just couldn't get up those rickety little stairs that led to the attic room. As soon as I could, I painted this room black – floor, ceilings and wall. I put a hammock in the middle of two low-hanging beams and then, when I had the money, I had a special projector put in.

As I lay in that hammock, floating in my black room, the projector would begin to show the different planets and stars. I would lie there, the solar system in front of me – some of the planets and stars were in 3D. This is where I find true solace and peace. Sometimes, I would lie and look at planet earth looming directly over me. Sometimes, I would lie there and just see

watch the stars and the planets in the back ground. This space room is my grounding room. I had come here when I had successfully shown Nana's friends that she was no longer fit for purpose – it was a very surreal moment, lying there in the dark, watching the planets and stars whilst I listened to Samuel Barber's "Adagio for Strings". It was the fulfilment and peace that I had needed to gain back my calm.

I sense you are beginning to doubt my powers and fail to understand the damage I can do. Once again you lose faith so quickly, and once again I have to show how great I am.

So as a small flavour of my capabilities, let me tell you about our family trust manager: Derrick Osbourne.

Derrick was a much loved and trusted man of our little town. Nana loved him. She loved that he too was a descendant from the original families, and I much suspect she had wanted her precious daughter to marry him.

I hated him! He reeked of slime, of a false importance. After the Robin's eggs incident, Nana had acted on her threat to disown me and scuttled off to meet with Derrick. It didn't take me long to hack into his system. It was easy for me to see that Nana truly had kept to her word and cut me off. Now, if this had happened to you I am sure you would have cried, but not me. It got me thinking, and it didn't take me long to come up with a plan.

I prepared well by taking time to think over a nice cup of tea, and within twenty minutes of looking into his details I saw that darling Derrick was out most Friday nights under the pretence of walking the dog and giving his wifey some "me time". I found that local boy Derrick was actually a frequent member of the local dogging sites. In those days, I wasn't even that good at hacking into people's systems, but I had managed to do it via a simple hack into his wifi. Can you believe the dimwit used his date of birth as a passcode? His wifi was also aptly named the "Osbourne's wifi", which made it so easy for me to work out which one it was that I wanted to hack.

Within one week, I had worked out how he planned his "dog walks" and I planned my next moves accordingly. I planned my stalking events for all the local sites I could get to easily without being caught. I hacked into as many of the council's CCTV units as possible, but not all were easily hackable and the picture quality was very poor.

Nana had been suspicious as to why on Friday nights I had suddenly become excited about going out. As she was now scared of me, she didn't dare comment openly, but I am sure she mumbled something about the apple not falling far from the tree. I was in Ninja mode and decided to let her off with that one. She would suffer the consequences soon enough.

It didn't take me long to get what I needed. In those days when I was still learning, I had to go out and do some field work to get some lovely graphic evidence in the form of photographs and videos of Derrick masturbating outside somebody's car whilst he leered into it. It is funny how little people notice what is going on around them when engrossed in filth. The texts and emails were much easier for me to get.

I always came back and made sure I washed thoroughly after these spying events. Once, it was so horrible just listening to the grunts and human filth that I almost wretched out loud.

Once I had gathered what I needed, I made an appointment to see Derrick. I could hear the smirking and smugness in his voice as he spoke to me and leered at me over his desk. Pretentious bastard! That word makes me shudder. He was a fool for thinking I was a stupid spoilt rich kid who hadn't realised that the family estate was signed off to the local cats and dogs home.

I had sat there quietly, letting him have his false glory as he puffed his chest out and spoke to me about how he felt sorry for me and how he had been close to my mum. Now, if I wasn't mistaken – I am not sure – but was there a glimpse of regret in his eyes when he spoke of Abi? It was gone fast – he carried on with his monotone drone about how it was such a shame she had chosen the path she had. If I was ever proud of Abi, then this moment would be it. Well done to her for rejecting this creature.

I sat and watched him, almost without blinking. I kept the stare to the same intensity and soon he realised. When he realised that I was just staring at him and not speaking, he started feeling nervous. Slowly, without taking my eyes off his oddly-shaped, spongy face, I took out the evidence from the file I had in my hand. I started to place the photographic evidence on his desk. One incriminating item at a time.

Now it was my turn to bask in the glory. To feed off the power rush that was bubbling inside of me, as he grew weaker at the realisation of what he was looking at.

"Where? ... Where? .... What? ... Who? ..." He stood up and leaned toward me, to intimidate me, but I sat there tall, using my height and my unfaltering stare. I didn't flinch once. I sat still facing forward as if I was frozen.

He sat back down and looked me straight in the eyes. He tried to stare angrily at me, but he couldn't do it. Little pampered

Derrick didn't have that kind of nerve. He started to rub his head. He blinked profusely and picked up one of the print outs of his sordid request emails to a couple he regularly watched. He stood back up and he paced about the room and banged his fist onto a wooden filing system.

He cursed at me, "You're stupid and crazy – I will prove that this … this is all fake. God, half the town knows there's something not right about you. Your own grandma … I …"

It was my turn to speak.

"If you like, I could send this to your wife, or perhaps the school where your children are? You see, even if you prove them to be fake, which you can't, you will be ruined. You know how it is in Valhan – they will have the Village hall up and running within minutes to offer support with tea and cakes to everyone."

Derrick stood up again and walked out of the room. I could hear his panicked breathing, a sound that made me rather happy.

I sat there and waited for him to come back and start pleading.

That was the day I had Nana's will changed, making sure that everything was left to me. I had also not so

politely assured Derrick that I had enough evidence to bring him crashing down, and now that he had changed Nana's will, I would use that little piece of evidence too, to destroy him professionally as well as personally. I am sure I heard the weakling whimper as I left.

It wasn't about the money or the house, you see. It was the principle of it all. I had enjoyed showing Nana her altered Will. I had enjoyed watching her crumple. I loved the look of resignation that cast over her frail face.

You must understand, I was only starting out on my journey at the time when I encountered Derrick. I am much more powerful now. My online streams cater to a population that would create their own country, not a town or a city: an entire country!

My journey has made me interact with some very powerful people online and they respond and respect me more than Valhanians do for now.

My daily routine is simple. I have Martha, the cleaner, who comes in daily to keep the house spotless. I can't abide a dirty house, and although I clean it better than she ever could, I like the smell of the house after she has finished with it. Martha makes her own solution passed down to her from her great aunty, and it has a wonderful lemony fragrance. I go for a jog and my run finishes at the same time Martha finishes cleaning. I usually go for a shower, then we share a cup of tea whilst she discusses the local gossip, and then she leaves. I have got the timing down to a T.

Martha was the cleaning lady at school. She suffered worse jibes from the snobs than I had. Martha is

European and Nana hated her. Martha was always kind to me. When I had started to take on the reins and made Nana despondent, I had hired Martha. Nana was furious with my choice, but didn't dare argue with me. Martha knew that my study was off limits and she never asked any questions. Nana hated the day I had installed a highly efficient, but not so subtle lock for the study door. She was furious at the amount of packages that came, delivering me screens, units, desks and more screens. Nana's eyes had scrutinised the deliverymen who bought everything, but she was too scared to say anything. When she would spot Martha, Nana would turn her nose up and flounce off in the opposite direction.

Martha is professional. She gets the job done. Which is why more and more people locally hire her. She is kind but not clucky and I prefer that. It boded well for her that she never asked me any questions but kept me up to date with the locals.

It was from Martha that I heard that Nana's friends were worried about her when she had stopped attending the social club a few years back. It was from her that I learnt that they were also worried about me coping, and apparently they were quite split in their judgements. Half the town think I am a lost child and won't manage the estate and monies that I would inherit; the other half admire me and have done some research on my work, the My First Teddy app – they know I will be fine. A huge majority of them talk about the fact that I am single and it is about time I should settle down, get a family and children to keep me grounded. However, Martha was not only for me to gain insight about the locals' gossip. Initially, when I was working on my outcome for Nana, I had used Martha to put out messages I wanted people to hear. You see, I am charming like that and Martha was my messenger because I know she loves to talk. During our chats, with a cup of tea in hand, I had told Martha how Nana's mental health had deteriorated and she was getting confused and paranoid. I told Martha that the only reason I was allowed to do my degree at home was because leaving Nana alone would mean she may harm herself. As her only living family, I couldn't possibly put her in a home. I showed Martha some self-inflicted bruises on my arms and told her that Nana had hit me a few times out of confusion. I had to keep the hitting lies low key, otherwise I would have the social services knocking on the door and that was one thing I did not want. I had learnt Martha's native dialect of Hungarian and used certain words to emphasise the importance of not letting too many people know as a backup.

Martha had served her purpose well. All of Nana's local friends knew of her deteriorating mental health. They knew she had sudden outbursts of anger and rage, and this scared everyone. I remember one day Cynthia and Shone had come over. Nana was confused from the sleeping tablets I had given her. She fell asleep on her couch, snoring quite loudly and waking up confused. Cynthia had cried at her friend's health, but Shone had nudged her mum till she stopped crying whilst not so subtly raising her eyebrows towards me.

Back to today. I had to give up my run as I couldn't be seen out running on the day of the service. As I am drinking my tea with Martha, she tells me that Derrick was looking to speak to me about some unfinished estate business. He had come to the service to talk to me.

This infuriates me. The coward! He came to talk to me in a room full of people so I couldn't manipulate him. The coward couldn't face me, so he came and found my maid.

I am angry!

I also can't believe there is anything outstanding. I had covered all the bases, or so I had thought. I have enough of my own wealth to buy myself a million of these types of properties, but I'm furious that the old witch had

perhaps got one over me and managed to stick a finger up at me from beyond her ashes.

My face has ignited into a huge ball of fire from the anger!

I stand up and see the fright on Martha's face. I ignore her and she flinches as I storm past her.

I am running upstairs and into Nana's room. It was once my mother's room, but after her precious daughter had passed away, Nana had moved in. It was a disgusting blend of a young girl's pinky-peachy fantasy bedroom that reeked of an old person's musty smell. She had never allowed me into the room, nor allowed Martha to clean it. This was going to change – I throw open the curtains and throw open the windows. I start to pick up anything I can get hold of and start to hurl it out of the window. Photographs, jewellery boxes, little ornate baskets with toiletries, clothes, bed sheets and pillows. I stop. I take a huge breath of fresh air. I exhale slowly and look around at the disarray of clothes, photos and books. I see a funny-looking purple book with a pen attached to it. How incredibly ancient! Who even has those now? I pick it up to hurl it out of the window, but a photograph falls out.

It is my mum – she looks happy. She is wearing a cream dress with red flowers on it. She is standing with Shone – she looks happier than I have ever seen her in photo. The only photographs Nana had shown me were formal ones. I flick through book and realise that it is my mum's diary. Now you all know that I am not sentimental, but there is something about this diary that stops me from throwing it – I could pass some time reading this and then enjoy burning it, or perhaps I will keep it to remind myself never to be weak, for I can assure you the words written in this diary will be as weak as the human who wrote them, the sort of human that is filled with all sorts of emotions and longings that make me want to throw up on the best of days.

I am back in control. I stand tall and breathe. I hold onto that diary like it is reminding me of why I am where I am today.

"Martha!" I command. She is here fast. I like that about her. She won't look up at me. Her head is down and her hands are clasped. "I want this room gutted out. Everything can go to charity or the bin."

Martha doesn't dare look up and she replies with a steady voice in her usual broken English, "Yes, I will sort you." She still doesn't dare look up.

"I want it cleaned out and painted white within a week. And use people who will not make a noise." With that, I nod and walk upstairs to my haven.

A while later, after some calming time with some mantra music, I descend back to my study.

I start to stream Osbourne and Son: Legal and Financial Services. I scan all their screens till I can see that weasel Derrick. He is looking perplexed, so I decide this is the best time to call him.

His face is petrified when he sees that it is I who is calling him. I can see the doubt creep over his porous face as he decides on what to do. Finally, the creep sees sense and answers my call.

I decide to speak first using my best monotone voice.

"Derrick you needed to speak to me." I purposely make this a statement and not a question.

I watch him looking even more nervous and he pulls something in from the side of his desk. It looks like an envelope and paperwork; the angle from his computer isn't letting me see exactly what it is. I try logging onto his phone view, but I get a shot of his waxy ears instead. I wait for him to reply.

"Well, uhm err … usually err … I am meant to do this face to face and, eh … eh …"

"Derrick, you don't want me as your enemy now do you?"

I quickly start hacking into Derrick's personal computer

history and a quick ping on my system shows he recently paid for a transaction involving live porn.

I watch him and hear him trying to construct a sentence whilst I am typing furiously.

"Well, you know it … err … is something your gran left. I only got it … she left it … eh … errr … with her friend. I've not even opened it and I reall–"

I don't let him finish. I really don't have time for his bullshit.

"Derrick, would you like me to send your wife a detailed shot of you giving yourself a little treat? Derrick, just send it to me. You do whatever you have to so that this situation is above board and aligned to what we discussed, but if I don't get this new stuff, whatever it is, sorted by the end of today, your wife will be getting a nasty little surprise. Do you understand?" I add, "If anything needs signing, send it to me too. I will check it all and send it back to you." Now I lower my voice to a slow, seething, hissing noise. "You do not come to me Derrick, if you know what's good for you! Have it sent to me. Oh, and check your mail – I believe you have a new message."

With that, I hang up. I watch him open up his personal e-mail. It is from one of my fake accounts. It is a short video taken from his personal computer showing Derrick's twisted face as treats himself whilst he watches two girls and a boy pleasure each other in sick ways.

Derrick is quickly trying to close it down, delete it. He looks sick. He is sitting at his desk with his head in his hands. How stupid can you get? Doesn't the fool realise the urgency of the matter. I send him a text from one of my many numbers.

"Don't forget the deal – end of TODAY!"

I watch him panic again as he reads the text. He calls his secretary and barks orders about sending a courier to my house.

I sit back and wait.

# CHAPTER FIVE

A flurry on my screen shows me that a courier has arrived at Derrick Osbourne's Office. His secretary gives him his instructions and he leaves.

I have a 20-minute wait. I pick up the diary and start to read it from where there is another photograph, this time Mum with Shone – the photograph is almost like a bookmark, posting me to the right pages:

*Today was awful! Not only was mum in a foul mood with her caterer and myself over some silly mistake over cakes at her stupid tea party but that awful Derrick pestered me all the way from school. He kept pawing at me and telling me my hair was like magic. He makes me sick, but he won't stop pestering me no matter how much I tell him. I can't believe my own mother thinks we should hook up. He is awful.*

In the margin there is a hand drawn picture of a round face, with a stick figure that is labelled Derrick, who is running toward a hole in the ground whilst a stick figure of two girls labelled Shone and Abhi look on.

I never knew much about my mum Abi, but the sense that I got from Nana and stories from Shone was that she was head strong and my so called "bastard father" had destroyed her ability to think straight. I read on intrigued.

*Shone and I are going to go to the Crackle Heath bowling alley. It will keep us out of sight from my Mum's nosey pals and apparently*

*Crackle Heath is full of hot college guys. Can't wait to see some decent looking guys and not just slimy Derrick and the rest of the boring Valhan guys. Shone has set it up so it looks like we are going to a field trip to support us with our homework, Oh god, I am so excited, What should I wear?"*

Here she has drawn a picture of a happy face and her name written in different ways. Like she is trying to find her signature. She has started neatly: going down line by line, but with each attempt you can see the laziness creeping in.

I go to put the kettle on. I keep pressing the lever to reheat the water every time it goes off. I don't make the tea just yet.

The CCTV camera sends me the alert that someone is outside, breaking my trance – I have a glance at the monitors in the kitchen. Finally, the courier has arrived. I watch him. His bike is struggling slightly on the gravel as he enters the driveway. I open the door before he can ring the doorbell – he looks at me like he is expecting me to give him some sort of homecoming welcome, a red carpet perhaps? Stupid moron. He gives me a small package and starts pointing a handheld device and giving me instructions to sign something. Before he can push that ghastly germ riddled machine at me, I tell him I will sign and deliver it myself when I am ready. He doesn't understand that I Am God, that I can do these things. He starts to protest but I take the parcel from him and tell him to sort it with Mr Osbourne. I walk into the house, slamming the door behind me.

I watch the courier on the monitor in the hallway. Standing there with his slightly raised hands and elbows pointing at his hips. He shrugs and shakes his head, then kicks a few gravel stones in defiance, sticks a finger up at the closed door and pushes his bike away. I press the kettle lever again as I walk past it and I sit down, whilst thinking that the kettle and its bubbling water reminds me of me in so many ways.

I open the small stuffed parcel, dread running through me. There is a copy of the will – the will that I had put together, so that is some relief. There is some paperwork for me to sign – that too is fine. Lastly, there are some envelopes. I don't like surprises. This isn't expected. I walk into the kitchen and make myself some long-awaited tea using fresh water.

I look at those envelopes like they are going to sprout an alien head and attack me. I drink my tea and prepare myself. I like organisation, so I place them all out on the old wooden table that has been in my family for generations. Nana didn't have to protest about keeping this. I actually admire the craftsmanship.

I place the envelopes by order of handwriting. There are three that are not Nana's handwriting. There is just one with Nana's handwriting. The envelope itself is thick like it's full of something. The last one is the smallest envelope, which I find hidden between the others. I decide to start with the smallest.

It contains a note. I can tell the envelope has been tampered with, like the person who had opened it had tried to reseal it. I would place a bet on the fact that the no-good Derrick had a nosey around it before he gave it me, but I know he would be too scared to look inside anything that was meant for me. It is addressed to my mother. No stamp – but fully addressed – I wonder if it was hand delivered at the time?

The handwriting is messy but readable:

*Abi, this has been hard for me to write: when we first met, I should have told you I was married, although we shared some fun moments I can't leave my wife and child. I am not sure how you got pregnant. Are you sure it is mine?*
*I think it is best if you get rid of it and live your life. Dave.*

Well I wasn't expecting that. Funnily enough, it doesn't bother me as much as it should. He called his baby "it". How easily he as written those words " get rid of it" Now if this had been you, I can see you would fall apart. I can see how it would make you cry and make you dizzy like someone had pulled the floor from beneath you, but not me. I've had enough displays of weakness today to last me a lifetime.

I take the cold-hearted note and crumple it. I take a sip of my tea and breathe.

Next, I go for Nana's envelope. It is, unlike the others, still sealed and is addressed to that excuse of a man:

Derrick Osbourne.

I open it and laugh recklessly as I read her first paragraph:

*Dear Mr Derrick Osbourne,*

*I have left this with my friend Celia. She has been instructed to give you this should something happen to me. Please understand and accept that this is my final will and testament:*

*My wicked Grandchild has been devious and crafted a fake will. I don't know how this has been achieved.*

*I am scared to come and give this to you in person for fear of being seen and punished.*

*Every day, I live in fear and as a prisoner. Celia has come by today and has agreed to bring you this letter. Celia was unsure about taking any responsibility, as she didn't believe me when I told her about my living conditions and she politely told me to see a doctor to help me get back to my old self. I am not sure why she thought something was wrong with me. She kept her distance from me like I was crazy. She was however polite enough to wait for me to write this.*

*I know that you will rectify my Will according to my wishes. I cannot let that demon live in my ancestral home.*

*I also wish for you to destroy these letters. I had originally wanted them passed on, but now I no longer care. I cannot destroy them here without being found out.*

*I thank you and your family for being such good support to me through some of the toughest moments in my life.*

*I wish you well.*

Then she has signed off with her characteristic signature. Oh my days! This has made me laugh hysterically. This is my family: one tries to rip out my heart, the other fills it with amusement.

I will stand strong and not allow my blood to do this to me. I will no longer allow it.

I stand straight. I laugh at her silly copy of the will that wants to leave everything to the pesky animals. Whilst Celia was the only one who had ventured over to meet Nana now and again, she was like everyone else, she

believed the lies about Nana and her fragile state of mind.

Nana's letter and the original will are now crumpled and lie scattered across the table alongside the crappy note from the man who is my father.

Now it is the turn of the last three envelopes. They are old and tattered. It makes me wonder why Nana had wanted me to see them at first, but had then changed her mind.

I pick up the one closest to me. *Person unknown at this address* is written across it. I look at the rest – it is the same for all of them. Two of them have been addressed to different addresses, one to a David Harvey, the last one just to a Mr David.

I look at the dates of the stamps across the front, sort them by date and open the first one.

*To My Love Dave,*

*I hope you are well. I write to you in the hope of reaching out to you. The last couple of months have been the best of my life. I never dreamt that I would meet someone as wonderful as you.*

*I am not sure why you left so suddenly. I am not even sure if you heard me when I told you I was pregnant.*

*I know I have told you that my mother is strict and very old fashioned, but she is keen to meet with you. I always thought that mum would not understand but she does and I am so ecstatic. I am not scared any more and your love gives me strength to face the world and mum wishes us to be married before the baby is born.*

*I miss you! I miss talking to you and being close to you. I wish I could somehow bring you back to me.*

*I don't even know if this is the right address for you. I tried looking for your name in the yellow pages, but now when I think of it I am not sure if you are from the local area. I do hope I have got*

41

*the right address.*
  *Please do write back. I shall look forward to meeting you again.*
  *I miss you every single day.*
  *forever yours,*
  *Abi.*

Seriously, how pathetic is my family? Don't lose faith in me people, as the people of my family show you how weak they are. Let me tell you I am never going to be weak. I am the strong one, the one that will not break down at every given corner. Once again, I crumple this letter and add it to the other pile.

The second letter is just as pathetic – Abi declaring her undying love to David, worried she has the wrong address. But her last letter is probably the most pathetic.

*Dear Dave,*
  *This is my last letter to you. Mum and the midwife have said it will help me get closure and move on. I gave birth to our beautiful baby last week, but I cannot hold it or feel any happiness. The baby looks like you. The same dark hair and beautiful brown eyes. For the last few months, I have had to endure the taunts from my mum for being stupid in believing in you. For being stupid to have fallen with child before marriage. I feel so numb and so lost. I hope that nothing bad has happened to you. Now I realise that I may not even have your last name right. Mum said that you are already married. I have no idea what gives her this crazy notion. I just need to let you know that your love is the best thing that has happened to me and now I have nothing. Since the day my dad died my life had been a misery and then I met you and it all changed. We have a child together. It was born from our love but I can't love our child without you beside me. Most days I don't even know what day of the week it is. The nurse said I may be suffering from some form of depression but I know I will be better as soon as I see you again. Please come back to me and show my mum that you are not married and that I am not wrong.*
  *I miss you every minute of the day now.*

*Love from your Abi.*

Stupid cow called me "it". I am starting to feel a new sensation, like some form of cold liquid is seeping through my veins and settling in fast and hard. I like this feeling. It is making me feel strong. My mother, she fell in love with a man whose bloody name she didn't even know, a man who wanted me dead. No wonder Nana hated him. I understand parts of her hatred now. A part of me has died inside, that one hope that perhaps one day a father would come to rectify his wrongs. But he is a coward and a cheating bastard – that nasty word again, the one that makes me shiver – who took advantage of a lonely girl.

I walk over to the other log burner in the side of the kitchen beside the newly installed folding doors. I light it up and I wait till the fire is burning bright, and that is when I throw one damned letter in at a time. Those silly letters that had weakness written on them. Weak people with weak thoughts that deserve nothing but the wrath of the fire. I watch the fragile paper curl up and blacken, the blackness spreading like an agressive cancer and eventually taking over its host and destroying everything. This is the end of that era; this is now the start of a new time. From the burnt charred paper a new spirit arises, showing me what I must do.

I Am God. I Am God – I will not be affected by your stupidity or by your lack of belief. I Am God, I will create a new path for myself.

I am going to make myself another cup of tea. I also begin to read her diary. She mentions meeting Dave and some details about how wonderful he is but then suddenly it stops and the diary has no more entries. The entries seemed to stop as soon as she tells Dave about her pregnancy. The previous entries are mostly about her escaping Derrick who is persistently pursuing her. There are some drawings and some scribbles with Abi and Dave in love hearts, but no more writing.

I have this feeling of frustration and hate not having control. Nana, as miserable as she was, still allowed me to have that control and since she has gone I am starting to feel a strange restlessness, one that I know I can calm if only I get back to where I need to be. I need to regain some control.

As I take in the last sweet warmth of my tea, my mind begins to wander. I am creating a new path and as the idea begins to form, I feel an excitement. I have a country worth of people at my fingertips. I wonder if I could try out a small experiment. You will love it, of course! You all are addicted to real-life trashy reality shows – then why not help me by being enthralled in the one that I am about to create? I Am God after all and it's about time I got practical and stopped dwelling.

As my plans begins to formulate, I head up to see how Martha is getting on. She stands upright when she hears me come in. I ignore her for now. I don't look at her. I start rummaging through my mum's clothes. I find what I need. Martha looks perplexed when she sees me standing with the dress I have picked up. It's almost like she feels that I am going to strangle her with it. I smile my

fakest smile and walk off without an explanation. She nods slowly, but doesn't look too convinced. God I hate people. I tell her to get on with it whilst I walk out of the room. I go to my room to go and get ready for a run. I no longer care about what the people of Valhan will say.

# CHAPTER SIX

My systems are all set up in such a way that it is running automatically. I don't need to do the hard work anymore. My system streams everything that I need. I have coded it all to perfection, of course. I also have a small team dotted around Asia and the US that manage the My First Teddy app. I prefer it this way – no contact, just some online discussion and a few video conferencing meetings. This way I can justify most of the money that comes into my accounts. Of course for me it's amusing to see what the staff really think of me. I can see what they type about me all the time on their WhatsApp group that they have set up without me. All I will say is; that it is a good thing I'm not easily offended, although I do enjoy manipulating their lives. I fire them and then make sure that their CV never gets sent out to any firms. I make sure it is lost in cyber space. One of my ex staff who was particularly nasty about me, Abrim, well he committed suicide after spending a year trying to get a job and not understanding why no one called him back. I then enjoyed clearing out his bank account. The idiot did everything online. It was so easy getting hold of his passwords. When he sent his letters of complaint via email, I made sure they also took a detour, never deleting them, so they continued circulating cyber space. I had loved watching the despair on his face, every time he checked and made phone calls, not understanding why he was getting no response. I had fed off it. He was a true weakling though and gave up the fight for his life quite quickly. Choosing the cowardly movement of  stepping in front of a moving train. His family were devastated. He had been one of the first children to have got an education and then go on to get a well paid job, that provided a steady income. They were a poor family that had sold their failing farm land and lived in a small hut, using their humble savings to educate their children. So when Abrim got his first job, his income helped support the household, the younger siblings' education and also helped his parents increase their status and bragging rights in their community. It turned out he was only a big mouth key board warrior and not so brave after all. His messages about me were based on all things he could do to me if he ever met me and how easily he would win in a real life face to face. Weakling.

Once Abrim had died – I, of course only found out officially via one of the chats and straight away I took my role as his employer seriously. I sprung into action and set up a fund to send his family some money to help support them. His mother sent me a message of how when god takes with one hand, he gives with the other.

I had sent them enough money to cover 20 years of Abrim's salary. Every year his siblings send me photos of their success, telling me they couldn't have done it without the support of their saint. I also ensured the bank got Abram's emails eventually and his story was leaked to local media, then published locally. His mother had cut out the news stories and kept them in an album. They talk a lot about how if only his emails had arrived to the bank and had the bank sorted out the mistakes on his account, he would not have died.

I look at all the screens. I can see everything. It's like seeing all your TV channels on different screens, and like TV, these days nothing appeals. I almost start behaving like you humans and start to flick through the screens one by one. I am also working on my keyboard, drumming in variations of names and codes. I have this inbuilt screen on my bench, so it's mostly me drumming my fingers on the table top. It is almost like playing a beautiful tune on a piano. I like it! The clickety click of the keyboard keys used to drive me insane after a while. My desk is like a huge touch screen – it was very advanced technology when

I had it built in.

Bingo! My search has worked because suddenly there it is: a face, so angelic and so familiar it almost takes my breath away. I wasn't expecting this, but there is something familiar that connects me to it. I click on the screen and make it bigger. There she is. She is laughing without any constriction. This is what makes me feel jealous. This is what has caught me off guard. I can't ever imagine laughing so freely. I start typing into my systems to get more of her details.

Registered details under a Mr D H Bailey. Well that clearly isn't her! I delve in deeper.

I am not sure what it is, but there is something so soft and beautiful about her face, there is a vulnerability that is drawing me to her. A vulnerability that makes me angry at her weakness, angry because it reminds me of a younger version of myself. Then there is a part of me that is curious.

She is laughing at a video sent to her, a video of her nephew playing with his My First Teddy bear on the newest Christmas edition of the app. Baby and Teddy can dress as Santa, sitting on a beautiful sleigh and you can make the reindeer look like the parents. As predicted, Rudolph is always the dad.

I see her laughing, and then she comes out of the app to look at her message. A message from someone called Chloe:

> CHLOE
> You ok?

A very apt sentence for a 15yr old girl. Emma types back:

> EMMA
> No fed up with the parents

Send. She types very fast.

> EMMA
> Arguing again! This evening's hot topic is the bins!! {Roll

eyes emoji} I never want to be old {old lady emoji}

CHLOE
Gawd {crying with laughter emoji}

Found her: Emma Bailey. Age 15. Her Facebook and Snapchat is telling me lots. Her  various check ins, the status updates, the pages she has liked. I even know that before she sleeps she listens to a bit of Justin Bieber or Olly Murs, depending on her mood. It's her most played tune on Alexa that surprises me – she loves a bit of Madonna's material girl. I wonder if her friends know?

I now know where she attends school, her house address and her local hang out with her friends. I told you,  I Am God. That didn't even take me 10 minutes.

Emma forwards Chloe the video with the message:

EMMA
my cute little baby keeps me going
{love heart, Baby face and face with Heart eyes Emoji}

It doesn't take me a long time, you see, to become an invisible companion in this girl's life. Between Emma's phone, and now Chloe's details, I have unravelled a lot. I know both these girls, their routine and their social circle very well.

Their Snapchats are revealing a lot more than Facebook. Emma seems the standard 15 year old. She is worried her parents are splitting up. And there's a boy, or  possible boyfriend, called Oliver who just wants sex with her and is trying to bully her into it, but she isn't ready. Well that's a surprise to me. Most kids do the deed and worry about whether they were ready or not later.

She is depressed – this is clear. Her messages to her sister-in-law Natalie, who she sees as a step-in mother
figure, and Chloe show clear signs of depression. Last week, Emma told Chloe she felt like just walking out and never coming back as she felt lonely and sad. I feel a strange sensation wash

over me and my plan forms faster than I had thought it would. I even surprise myself at times. I had thought I would have taken a little bit longer to be at this stage. I wonder if I could make it work. I Am God – of course I will make it work. I just need a few days of espionage and then I will strike.

So allow me to let you in on the plan:

Step one: Identify target – done.

Step Two: I need a character and profile to get in touch with Emma.
Enter George Elliot, my new creation. I swear you will love this guy. I already have a whole database accrued with pictures and profiles. I am always needing new identities to protect myself. I have many fake profiles, male and female. Digitally enhanced profiles to create trustworthy accounts.

Step 3: Make Emma fall in love with George.
Step 4: Make Emma do whatever I wish.

Emma Bailey will be my new experiment. For this one, even I will have to make some notes, because this plan is going to be different. It is going to give me the power surge I need to carry on, but as it is a different operating method for me, I have to ensure I get every detail correct so I can be prepared for when the finale happens.

It takes me ten minutes to understand what Emma does daily: walk to school, coffee shop, shopping, studying – lots of social media and mostly at night. Her conversations with her mother are declining. Her mother seems to be becoming a dictatorial type. Emma only ever responds with a yes, no or don't know with her dad. No wonder she feels so lonely. I am not empathising by the way; I am merely drawing a conclusion.

I spend another ten minutes mapping out where her local

haunts actually are and drawing a map of them. I am thoroughly enjoying myself – using a pen and paper is quite enthralling. No wonder Abi enjoyed doodling so much in her diary.

A further ten minutes to work out what motivates her and what makes her sad.

Another ten to reveal who her main influencers are – thank fully there are not many. So not too many         eliminations.

Then I spend a further ten minutes making a link to all her friends and creating her perfect soulmate: George    Elliott, my crucial pawn in this game.

Finally, the last ten minutes are used to make sure all bases are covered and that no one is left out. making sure that everyone she talks to, is linked to and related to are in this loop.

60 minutes and I am done – Project Emma is good to go. I stop and make myself some healthy lunch and a cup of tea.

I start to create my new social media profile. I know enough about Emma now to make George her soul-mate, her inner voice, her controller. I start trolling through the masses of faces in my portfolio. I look back at her likes and dislikes, what musicians and actors she likes, and I find the perfect face. I start to create a history for Emma's George, and start to make this face have a life. Perhaps the life I may have had – a family to moan about, a pet to hold on to. Happiness.

Please don't be fooled. I don't need your damn        sympathy. I need to use these stereotypes so that you can understand what I am creating. I look back at George's picture. He is cute, blonde, wavy longish hair, freckles, light eyes  and has just the type of face I am sure will hook Emma.

I create a Facebook page for my character and work on the date so that it goes back a couple of years. *You* can't do this because you only have basic user rights. *I* have more rights than some of the people who work for Facebook! I don't abuse it. I've only ever used it to my advantage. Power is a good thing, but it must be used responsibly and only someone like me can muster that strength.

I create duplicate Facebook accounts of Emma's not so close

friends and add them on to Emma's page. Yes, to answer your question, I am now logged onto her page. I am logged onto all the accounts I need to be. This also includes Chloe's, but right now I need to just focus on Emma. It is easy for me to add and delete what I want.

I link the duplicate accounts with my new profile. I make the settings on their pages so that only Emma can see them and no one else, and suddenly my new persona and Emma have a few friends in common. Distant friends that I know Emma wouldn't feel comfortable talking to, but whose presence will reassure her that the person I am creating is real and safe. Emma is not in a good place right now and creating someone who is a complete stranger to her would damage my progress. I have done my research. For this to work, I must have some familiarities that Emma can clutch onto for

support.

I have hacked into Emma's family through their electronics. I already know so much about them. I am becoming a regular fly on the wall in the both the Bailey households. I have access to the computers in Emma's room and the study. I have access to their smart TV, phones, all the Alexas, the CCTV systems outside their property, the dash cam on dad's car, both the Parents work computers and now access to both their companies' networks. Thank you, My First Teddy app. Thank you, Natalie, the clever sister-in-law who uses it frequently to give updates to the entire family. I will focus more on Emma and less on Jamie and Natalie 's household for now.

So my new plan begins its course.

Emma is back home already from school. Where has this day gone? I had plans to send her some messages, but now I am behind thanks to my research. Nevermind, a plan well thought out is not a hindrance but an advantage. Only a couple of days ago I was engulfed by my history but now I will do everything to rectify this and make sure that it is a history that no longer defines me or controls me. I have taken the reins and I will make the moves.

I am a digital ghost in Emma's house. She is home alone. Her dad is at work and her mum is out shopping and not working today.

Emma is talking on her phone and tapping her iPad simultaneously. She is flicking through fashion pages and Instagram whilst discussing the impending doom of her A-levels – I easily tap into her conversation: oh come on, don't you remember children, giving me access to your audio controls? You know that message that pops up "So and so app would like to access your microphone"? How quickly you press allow without understanding.

Emma is worried that she is going to fail her A-levels. She needs to pass them. She sees them as a way to get out of the house. The similarity to my situation is uncanny. Although I used my education to escape the   abusive   torture from Nana, whereas Emma can't stand her      parent's constant bickering – a different form of torture it would seem. She appears to be emotionally fragile. How can bickering make you so weak? She has no idea little miss princess.

Apparently, her parents had an argument this morning – oh boo hoo. Her dad left for work and his last comments were along the lines that coming home was "just awful" for him and "right now sleeping in the office chair would be like heaven". I had missed Emma's little breakdown. I had only seen her write it in a text to Natalie, but after writing all about being fed up and lonely, Natalie had not replied. I will need to be more vigilant. I need to be there when she is feeling her most vulnerable – this is the way I can get her to trust me and make it easier for me to control her. I can help ease the loneliness she feels. I am intrigued though, as to why she did not send the  second text she had written to her sister-in-law. I wonder if she feels she is being a burden to her? Natalie does not respond so quickly to Emma's messages. I don't think it is malicious. I think it is more about Natalie just being busy with her baby, Jamie and her own life.

I am accessing George's accounts. I need to increase the pace of this plan. As the good old saying goes, strike whilst the iron is hot.

# CHAPTER SEVEN

I decide to target her via Twitter first. Emma uses Twitter to express herself a bit more freely compared to any other social media outlet. Although, unlike most people who use Twitter, she is using her own name, but with a cartoon picture of herself. I find one of her posts about some makeup video that is trending. Emma has commented about the use of too much makeup destroying young people's self esteem. This is the tweet:

> Videos like this put too much pressure on girls like me. I'd love to be #makeupfree but find it so hard    because of the constant pressure to look perfect.

Total of 154 character count on Twitter.

I find the tweet out of character for Emma because, from what I know, she does as she is told. She wears makeup because it is expected of her. I like this little show of backbone, it empowers me knowing that I will easily break her. You can have the fun of watching me do it.

I wait till she is online and only type when she is on Twitter. I need her to be on Twitter and reading it live. I can't trust or leave it to fate for her to follow up a

notification. My patience is rewarded. She is online and on Twitter, so I find the tweet and first I press the little heart at the bottom of her tweet to show I like it and now for George's first tweet:

> Nice to see a girl so anti makeup – wish more girls were like

you.

I see her face as she reads it; I see the smile. A simple message to cheer her up, a simple message to lure her in. Loneliness is a funny thing, isn't it? Sometimes it makes you do things you would have sworn off. Loneliness combined with social media is a dangerous thing, it leaves you open to so many dangers. Twitter has about 200 million regular users, if not more. Behind all those faces there could be anyone and, in some cases, people will never know who it really is that they are talking to. Emma is about to find out soon enough though. Just be patient.

She is clicking into George's Twitter profile and checking out his pictures. She focuses on one; I can see how long she is actually looking at the pictures, how many seconds per picture. I can see her primative reactions to each picture very clearly.

My new social media set, face book, Instagram, snapchat twitter and anything else that you can think of is targeted towards her. I've created George for her. George has liked and been to the same places she has and has also tweeted similar tweets. He is also fed up with life because his parents are miserable. George is her, but in a male form. George also has a few friends in common. Do you see? Do you see what I did? How easily I'm going to come into her life.

I see the picture she seems to keep going back to. It is George picking up a dog and doing a fun selfie. I can understand why she likes it. George looks good. George is a face made up of facial mapping of many men and boys and created to appeal to the masses. I can see her smile as she looks at this pic. The dog was chosen very carefully from looking at Emma's posts, she has always wanted a dog and it seemed like the perfect lure to draw her toward me.

She hits reply and types:

aww thanks

She deletes this and retypes it about ten times before she sends her final reply:

> aww thanks {smiley emoji} #makeupfree

George types back:

> I know, I reckon my dog {insert pic of dog} looks
>
> better than most of these girls #nomakeupneeded

I can see Emma looking at the pic of the dog and smiling. She smiles a lot and now looks younger. Then she raises her head and looks towards the door. Her smile has gone now, replaced with a frown. Emma puts her phone down.

She walks towards the door and closes it and sits with her back to the door and covers her ears. I am watching her through her computer in her room.

I start typing into the programmes and see her dad is logged into his smart TV. The TV is on so that makes my life a lot easier. I turn the camera on and see what is going on.

I see her dad sitting on the couch. I have watched him a lot, he intrigues me. He is highly selfish and mainly just wants to come back from work and sit and do nothing but flick through the channels, whilst scrolling through his phone. His wife can't seem to let him do that. Today he looks weary and his shoulders are drooping. He is wearing formal suit trousers and a white shirt, sleeves rolled up and top buttons undone. Her mum is standing, looking harassed, with her apron on and holding stuff in her arms. She is shouting about how his jacket and work bag aren't going to hang themselves up and why there is a reason that there is a place for everything. He starts shouting back about being shouted at. He picks up the remote and switches channels and puts the volume up.

I can't help it but I have a programme that can allow me to stream whatever I like onto your television. I find their wedding song, "I will always love you" from *The Bodyguard*, and send in the stream. I see the look of confusion on both their faces. It makes me laugh. She looks at him, anger all forgotten, and smiles. A wistful look on her face. He looks relieved and confused at the same time. He gives the TV and the remote a look of thanks and breathes a deep breath of relief. He looks up at his wife and must be moved by some emotion as he gets up and hugs her. He takes the bag and jacket from her and puts them away.

A quick look at the other screen and I see Emma get up. She also looks relieved and she is back on her phone. She seems to have forgotten George right now and she is typing a message to Chloe.

> EMMA
> Today's argument seems to have piped down quickly. Wonder what happened?

> CHLOE:
> {prayer emoji} Use it as an excuse to get out. Come to mine.

> EMMA
> I'm already in PJ's {old lady emoji} maybe tomorrow. Xx

> CHLOE:
> K xx {love heart emoji}"

Emma flicks through her phone and finds the video of her nephew and watches it again and smiles. She sends her sister-in-law a message.

> EMMA
> our baby is too cute! {baby emoji}

Then she adds:

> Somewhat confused about what Christmas{santa emoji} is going to be like.

Natalie receives her texts and reads it. Yes, you have assumed correctly, I'm logged onto Natalie and Jamies' electronics too. Jamie does not do social media, but his wife loves it. Natalie reads Emma's texts and tells Jamie he really needs to speak to his sister. She says it in a nice way. Natalie seems to have a real soft spot for her needy sister-in-law. Interestingly though Natalie does not respond to the text straight away. Jamie is about eight years older than Emma.

Natalie mentions Emma's text content to Jamie and they both shrug and talk about how difficult Christmas always is. Natalie's parent's were never big celebrators of Christmas so generally they all ended up at the Bailey household where there was always a big tree, presents and Jamie's mum always added a special ornament each year, to help her remember some special events for that year. She also is one of those women who would crack easily if she didnt have matching plates, cutlery and glasses, so everyone always felt too on edge to actually relax.

Emma, seeing that Natalie hasn't replied is now going through her Snapchat – she makes faces, pouts and makes herself look like a dog with makeup on – snaps it and sends to Chloe.

> EMMA
> {pic} need to do this one together again #fun-times we had such a laff {crying with laughter emoji}

I am streaming pictures of "my dog" onto her Snapchat page replacing one or two of the ads. One of them finally catches her attention and then she remembers as she flicks over to Twitter.

Are you paying attention? Are you seeing what I am doing, how easily I can influence you? Just by changing a few of the tailored advertisements that the companies normally send you, I can control your unconscious brain. It is brilliant. Well actually, scrap that, I am brilliant.

Emma quickly swipes the feeds and then goes back to read George's messages. Once again she is stalking my pictures and reading my tweets.

She googles George's name and I send her a stream of data linking her only to my profiles. I don't want her to see any other real George Elliott. Only the modern-day monster I have created.

She hovers over my Facebook page and checks my status. I can see the soft smile on her face when she sees the word "single".

She is looking at my pictures again only this time on Facebook. I can't help myself as she is scrolling through George's photographs.

I press "like" to the picture she is looking at on her behalf. The look of horror and shame dawning on her face is far too funny; so I freeze the screen to watch her panic as she tries profusely to undo the damage. She's looking around the room for some help. I am watching her via her computer. She is sitting on her bed. She's now knocking on her phone, frantic movements of tap tap tap. I love this power. I need to lure her in so I can't scare her too much just yet.

So I unfreeze her screen and watch the relief wash through her, as she un-likes the picture and no doubt hoping that George does not see her like. Emma double checks to make sure she hasn't liked any of his other pictures. She slumps back onto her pillows with a sigh.

Back on Twitter George sends another message.

GEORGE
Hey sorry did my dog {insert pic of George and dog selfie} scare you? I didn't get a response?

I see Emma smile at the pic. She is back on Twitter now and smiling happily at the pic. Emma sends George a smiley emoji with the message:

EMMA
Dog is not frightening, owner may need a few filters – Sorry lol only j/k dog is cute

A sense of humour emerging. This is good as, from what I know, her humour pops up when she is nervous. This is a good sign for me. I am glad I make her nervous. I keep the conversation going.

> GEORGE
> Hey c'mon, well actually {dog emoji} keeps me from losing it at times. Do you have a dog?

> EMMA
> {roll eye Emoji} NO!!!! {Sad face and crying emoji}

> GEORGE
> Shame, dogs are the best. Mine's called Munchkin – hey I have sent you a DM – much easier.

> EMMA
> I would love one but parents won't allow it {crying emoji}ok will check.

I smile. Emma seems real and ready for a friendship. I can't help wondering how long it will be before I fully have her under my control.

I make George follow Emma on Twitter. I watch as she sees that George is now following her. She seems pleasantly surprised and happy. She goes into her DM's on twitter and find's George's message under message request.

> GEORGE
> Hey I hope you don't mind me emailing, you seem cool, unlike the usual girls I meet {roll eye emoji}

Emma has a look of mixed emotions from happiness and glee, but also worry. She starts to type.

EMMA
That's cool.

But she deletes it. After a few more futile attempts she sends George a{cool Emoji}. Nicely played Emma, she doesn't want to appear too desperate. Emma's finger hovers over the "follow back" button, but she doesn't. Interesting. Although I think I know Emma and I would have bet that she would have followed George back straightaway, she doesn't. Instead Emma checks her messages. There's a few group chat messages – her friends are discussing their latest homework assignments on WhatsApp and also who is going to wear what at the weekend. Emma responds to a few messages. She suggests they all get together and do a clothes swap, which is met with a great response from her friends.

Emma is happy and feeling very confident after that encounter with her friends. She rolls off her bed and starts ploughing through a huge pile of clothes before making a few selections. I can only gather she is going to take them to her friend's house for a swap. Emma gets up and stretches. She wearily goes to her door and creaks it open a little. She hears her parents talking in a low voice. They are actually sitting on the sofa cuddling, murmuring sweet nothings and stroking each other – it makes me sick just watching them.

Emma shuts the door softly and sits down on her bed. She picks up her phone and begins to do a few selfies. She goes into Twitter and goes through George's profile again. She goes into her WhatsApp and starts typing a message to Chloe.

EMMA
Hey, I have been followed by this cute guy on Twitter. Not sure what to do.

She looks at her message and then flits between it and George's account. She deletes her written message to Chloe and just sends her a stupid selfie and then goes back to Twitter and follows George.

This is enough for now. Tomorrow is another day.

I spend some time later watching her parents. Her mum is now pottering about in the kitchen. I tune into the sitting room. He is just sitting there on his phone again, the TV whirring quietly in the background.

He fascinates me. His posture, the way his hair falls down, the way he is slouched into the sofa like a giant human cushion.

He slowly raises his head up as if checking the coast is clear. He takes his work phone out from his pocket, and once again looks up towards the doorway before he unlocks it. My system shows me that he has a Skype chat message. It's from some user called "JJX". She has sent him a pic of them both together. He looks up quickly once again and then starts typing. He has given himself a three letter code name too:

SXY

Who took that? It's a nice one.

JJX replies and I watch the conversation unfold.

JJX
It was one of my friends, can't wait to see you Thursday eve.

SXY
I'm looking forward to it. I can't chat just yet. My ogre of a wife is watching what I am doing, speak soon love.

JJX
{kissy face emoji}can't believe you are with someone like her, honestly, she is horrid I still can't believe the way she talks to you. {sad face emoji} I will make you feel better when we meet.

SXY

{hugs emoji}I know you will. Can't wait to be with you. {aubergine emoji and winking emoji}

JJX

{blushing emoji, happy face emoji, love heart emoji}

I am not sure how to react to this. From the outside the Baileys look like the perfect family. Both parents have known each other since college, have fairly good careers, they live in a nice neighbourhood and have the perfect one boy, one girl family. Yet behind closed doors we have a mum who is a control and neat freak, a dad who seems to be having an affair with someone who is not only younger than him but incredibly beautiful, and then Emma, a very fragile and nervous young girl. Their son Jamie, seems to be the only one who has escaped unscathed? Or perhaps not, I can't look into this just yet, I am far too busy and far too occupied with Emma just now.

I do however save the photograph and a few others that I find in his Skype chat with JJX.

# CHAPTER EIGHT

I am frustrated this morning, I woke up with a strange fuzziness in my head but as I walk into my study my eyes hone onto my notes on Emma and I breathe. So far so good. She is playing into my hands.

I start to work on a profile I had made after I had created George. This is a profile of Lauree. She is an American blonde wanting to connect with a British guy because their accents are so sexy. She has been created to keep Oliver from harassing Emma. I need Lauree to keep Oliver busy and then I will connect all the pieces together. This little nugget came to me this morning when I was out for my morning run.

However, trying to connect with Oliver is slightly trickier. He isn't on social media as much as Emma and is actually quite a grounded guy, plays a lot of sports and video games. His favourite is a new craze amongst teenagers and addicted gamers called "Destination: Fire Pit". The game involves strategy and teaming up with like minded people across the globe, build your army to conquer and then rule the world known as: Fire Pit. Once you are ruler another army can come and conquer. Only one army can rule Fire Pit at a time, but it is almost near impossible to reach Fire Pit. My research shows that to get across one level, or nation as they call it on the game, can take up to two months depending on how strong your team is, which is why there are so many people playing it. The Myans Masters clan were the fastest to complete the first nation and have put up five hundred pounds worth of gaming gear for anyone who can beat their time record. Their You tube tips and cheats channel gets five     hundred times  more,  hits a day than any other Fire Pit Gamers channels.

To play you put together your team and then gain ranks – the higher the ranks the more chance of gaining better players. The person who creates the group can only ever be the leader, but there are other senior positions, top General, top Logisticians etc, and the leader cannot make key decisions without their support. High level troops and AI soldiers are bought and sold for skins, coins and stakes in some of the nations.

A very clever game, but it is not for me. I prefer controlling real people. Lauree will need to encounter Oliver in the game, I just needed to get her onto the group somehow.

I send a request to another user on a different platform of the dark net. I need him to infiltrate the group that

Oliver plays with, using Lauree's details. Oliver is part of an army called "Showcase Warriors". I send in my     instructions and wait.

I also check up on Emma. She is at school; her location services are always on so I can follow her about quite easily. She has sent some "secret selfies" to Chloe and gang via WhatsApp. They have a game where they are taking as many selfies as close as they can to a teacher without being caught. It is a funny game and if caught will most definitely result in detention and a whole two week ban from their phone. This is where the head teacher takes the phones  and puts them in her office and also threatens to sell it on e-bay if they get caught again.  Out of the whole group Chloe is definitely the most daring. Chloe's selfies are almost a whisper away from some of the teacher's, but Emma is a little bit scared, you can tell by her expressions on her face. I like that. I like that she has come from a family that have taught her discipline and respect. For me, this makes my job easier. "Do as you are told Emma, don't argue back Emma." She has been conditioned well from a very young age, to not argue back and not to make too much of a scene.

When Emma comes back from school she plops herself on her bed and calls one of her friends.

George is on twitter and sending Emma a direct message.

GEORGE
Hey, thanks for the follow back. Is Emma your real name or just a fake name for Twitter? George is my real name, real and old fashioned huh. I am so stressed, final year A-Levels {book emoji, geeky face emoji}.

Send.
I watch intently as she hears the ping on her phone and starts to try and put the call on speaker whilst she checks. She smiles at the notification and then tells whoever she was chatting to she will call them back. It isn't hard to make yourself important in a bored young person's life, you just need to know how to do it and pounce at the right time.
Emma smiles at George's message. This time she types quite quickly.

EMMA
Hey, I am in my first year for A-levels and it's pretty daunting. I am not sure if I will pass. Oh and name and pics are real.

She hits send. No retypes this time, no second thoughts.
George and Emma are having an in-depth discussion on Twitter direct mails about exams. George is clever. Funny isn't it how I can make him clever in the subjects that she is clearly struggling with, and how I can make him be the one who can help Emma with studying?

EMMA
I am struggling with Math. Are you a year ahead of me?

GEORGE
Yes, I am naturally quite good at Math, I promise I'm not showing off! Maybe I can coach you? I know how to study

for math and I have formulas that work. I have little tricks in how to remember them.

EMMA
omg {geek emoji} I would love to know! It would help me so much. I get muddled up quite quickly {monkey covering eyes emoji}My dad and brother are so clever, I always feel like the stupid one.

GEORGE
I can imagine it must be quite frustrating for you. Munchkin is trying to take my phone off my hand! I am sure he thinks it is a bone {insert pic of dog looking incredibly cute on bed sheets}

Thank you Photoshop, and all your other programmes that allow me to create this clever digital believable world.

EMMA
I am so jealous {dog emoji, love heart emoji} If you lived closer, I could have taken him for a walk.

She quickly deletes the love heart emoji and replaces it with {smiley emoji}.

George is suggesting that Twitter is too much hard work. Within twenty-four hours of our first contact Emma adds George as a Facebook friend and they have both exchanged numbers, George accepts the friendship request. I bet you didn't expect that, I bet you didn't expect that she would add me so quickly, but she has done. Welcome to the world of your children, where talking to strangers in public is frowned upon, but strangers on the internet is pretty acceptable. No, they are not going to tell you. I can read your mind. You can prepare them as much as you like, but kids will be kids. They will keep secrets. Ask yourself – go on. I Am God, I give you permission to look back at your youth and now tell me there were no secrets from your parents?

I can see Emma looking through my friends list. She hits mutual friends and looks surprised. She sends me a message.

EMMA

Hey, it looks like we have some people in common?

GEORGE

Hey, it is a small world. I am looking through them too. I think these people are friends of friends, but wow isn't that weird. Like we were supposed to connect or something.

Now comes the first step. The first ask. George begins to type a new message to Emma.

GEORGE

Emma, I know this is weird but I really need to ask a favour. I know we hardly know each other but it is so important.

George hits send.

Emma's face displays the perfect expressions; she looks worried, concerned and curious in that order. She begins to type back her reply.

EMMA

George, sure, is everything ok? Don't ask me for money though. Lol I don't have any!

I smile – she is joking, she is nervous. Good, a little bit of nerves will lure her in quicker. George types.

GEORGE

Emma, this is a big ask but it has freaked me out a bit that we have some mutual friends. I mean, it is good that we do have these friends. It kind of shows that we are real and normal people but I'm supposed to be focusing all my energy on my A-levels and my mum will go ape if she figures out that I have been chatting to strangers on this. I would appreciate if you didn't tell anyone about me, like your friends or family. You know what it is like. One person starts talking and then suddenly your folks find out.

I can't help chuckling. This should be an interesting one, to see if she is happy to keep me as a secret and also a sense check to see if she has told her friends, well mainly Chloe, about me. I know from looking at her messages that nothing has been said, but I need to know she has not verbally communicated anything.

I am watching Emma intently from her desktop. She hasn't responded as quickly as I had hoped for.

Once again she looks worried. This obsession with worrying is beginning to annoy me a little bit, for now I have to be patient. Like I was with the robins, the time will come when I will get my chance, but for now I will wait patiently.

She gets up from her bed and starts to pace. George is sending another message to ease her.

> GEORGE
> Babe, sorry. If my parents find out they will ban everything. I need my phone to help me escape from their constant arguing. I guess you might not understand what that is like but for me it is my escape – if this is too hard for you, we can stop talking I will understand.

Then for effect I write a third message.

> George
>
> It will be sad because I feel connected to you, but I will understand. I am too scared of losing my little bit of freedom, if my mum finds out.

Now I wait and watch.
Emma is still pacing. She is looking confused and this is

making me angry. I hate that she is so weak, that a simple request is perplexing her so much.

She sits back down on her bed; she is playing with her hair that's been pulled back in a messy bun. She's typing.

>EMMA
>Hey, what are your parents arguing about?

Silly girl. Answer the bloody question. God, I hate girls!! Now it is my turn to take a deep breath and type back patiently.

>GEORGE
>They argue over the silliest of things. I guess you will never understand as you probably have the perfect family, but mine will argue over who gets to sit where on a bloody couch.

>GEORGE
>Look, Emma I like you a lot. I can't risk losing my little bit of freedom that I have. I understand that you may need to tell your friends stuff, I respect that, but you have to respect my situation too and unless I have your word I can't really continue to chat with you. We know too many people in our circles that could get me into trouble.

Now I wait. The power of silence is a beautiful thing.

I start working on some of my other projects, checking that all the streams I've set up are working well. The user who I had asked to infiltrate Oliver's gaming group is chatting with me.

>Username Jello_47: Tried gaining access to Showcase Warriors in Game Destination Fire Pit. They are an advanced set of gamers: access or infiltration into this group is not going to happen. They have advanced quite far, they are well on their way to conquer Nation 4 and the leader is specific about who joins.

Username Jello_47: sorry buddy any other favours just ask.

I type back.

Username Code121: Thanks, no favours for now.

Today has been a day of twists and turns. I like the challenges. They are frustrating, yes, but they are keeping me sharp. I look at my notes and try to think of another solution. As I scroll through my notes I see it. This new strategy would mean killing two birds with one stone. Hah! I am such a genius at times it surprises even me.

I log on as Lauree and wait to start to start chatting with Adam. I connect with him on Sanp Chat for now it's easier to do this on a platform that allows messages to be deleted fast. He is Oliver's best friend, my backup guy, in place for Oliver in this tragic love story. It doesn't take long for Adam to respond. I am lucky that Adam plays nicely into my plan. What teenage guy is going to say no to an adventurous, blonde haired, blue eyed American. Your typical 'girl-next-door'. Especially one who loves British guys because they sound so cute.

Lauree starts typing.

Hey Adam, Its Lauree – sent with a very pretty pic of Lauree. Adam checks his phone, he is constantly on his phone and likes what he sees in Lauree.
Adam:
Hi, who are you?
Lauree:
Are you not Adam Dyrse from my class? Ashton College??

Adam:

No, where is that?
Lauree:
Michigan, Where are you?

ADAM:
England. I love American Chicks they are so hot.

LAUREE:
OMG {love heart eyes emoji} can I get a pic please… I will send you nice ones of me {smiley emoji} I love English guys OMG OMG I bet you have a real sexy accent.

ADAM:
Yes, I do I am from the posh part of my town. Sure…here's my pic {insert close up smiley face of Adam}

LAUREE:
Wow! is that really you? Very cute indeed {insert pic of made up Lauree with camera pointing down so you can see parts of her cleavage}
OMG I hope you like it. I am 17 years old. How old are you?

ADAM:
I'm 18. You are hot.{ emoji with toungue sticking out}

Adam is lying about his age. He has just turned sixteen, but he obviously wants to impress Lauree, I love it. He is far more carefree and naïve. He will be a quick win for me. Lauree types again.

LAUREE:
Really, you think I am hot? {smiley face emoji}

ADAM:
Yeh do you have a BF?

LAUREE:
No, I was hoping to hook up with some British guy, American guys just bore me y'know.

ADAM:
I'm English and single

LAUREE:
{insert pic of Lauree raising an eyebrow} wow!

Adam is overconfident and brash, he really has no tact or sense. He thinks by showing off he will get the girl. He is going to fall quicker than even I had anticipated and this is good for me.

My plan with Adam is to distract Chloe, I know Chloe has a huge crush on Adam. It makes me cringe to even think about crushes and closeness. Lauree will test Adam with a game based on reward.

After a whole hour of chatting, where the chat just gets downright lewd, Lauree starts to question Adam.

LAUREE:
Hey so if you really are 18 how come you don't have a girlfriend?

ADAM:
Ok... I am 17, I lied.

LAUREE:
I knew it. Have you even had sex yet?

ADAM:
Oh come on, yes! Loads of times. Have you?

LAUREE:
I bet you haven't...and yes.

ADAM:
Why would it make a difference? I know I would be so good at it.

LAUREE:
Ok so you don't have a girlfriend and you haven't had sex. When I come to the UK I want a guy who has a bit more experience.

ADAM:
We can do it over the net you know.

LAUREE:
That's not real you know, ok let's have a deal. Is there anyone at your high school who is into you?"

ADAM:
What do you mean?

LAUREE:
I mean is there any girl who likes you or that you might like?

ADAM:
Yeah there are loads of cute girls and I think a few like me.

LAUREE:
K, so what I want you to do is pick 3 girls that might like you and you might like and I will see what girl you can hook up with for practice, so that when you meet me you are ready.

ADAM:
Practice. Are you for real? You think girls are just going to have sex with me cos you chose them?

LAUREE:
No I will coach you how to get on with them and how to play the perfect BF and every time you do a good job I will send you some naughty pics of me.

Adam grins and almost drools at his screen, he just can't believe his good luck. He starts to type.

ADAM:
K so what do I need to do? I would love to see your naked pics {face with tongue emoji}

LAUREE:
So tell me bout these girls from your school, and I will find you the right one to start with.

ADAM:
K, so there are a few girls. There is one that my pal Oliver says is into me, a girl called Chloe, I like her. The other one I also like is Dawn, but she is hooked up with someone I think.

This is easy. I was not expecting Chloe's name to appear so quickly. I love it when life gets easy.

LAUREE:
Ok let's go with Chloe, do you know where she hangs out after school? Is there a park or something?

ADAM:
Yeh she is always with her pals either at the coffee and ice cream shop or at the park behind the school.

I love how kids these days disclose so much information online so easily. After coaching Adam on how to approach Chloe

I send him a shot of Lauree's breasts. He is beside himself. I promise to reward him eventually with some live footage but only if he can make it with Chloe and make it work. He is so happy. He has enlarged the picture I have sent him of some woman's boobs from the internet and is in hormonal teenager heaven. Later I will coach him on how to keep Chloe from being close with Emma, telling him to tell Chloe that he thinks Emma likes him, nothing like a bit of jealously to break a friendship.

Later on in the day, I see that Emma has started typing.

> EMMA
> George I feel scared

She deletes and then starts to retype.

> I am not sure, it is a big thing to ask. I don't keep secrets.

Delete.

> George, don't worry I am sure no one will find out.

Delete.

> George I am not sure what is worrying you? The friends we have in common are not that close to me. No one will find out. I think you are worrying for no reason.

Delete.

I like that I can see what she is typing. It is really helping me understand how her mind is working. She has stopped typing. I check her workstation in her room – she is not there. I tune into all the cameras and I see through her living room TV. She is flicking through channels and looking at her phone at the same time. She has changed out of her school uniform and is wearing grey joggers and a pink cami top. She looks cute and younger than her fifteen years.

Chloe has sent her a WhatsApp.

> CHLOE
> OMG, OMG are you free? Is your mum home? Need to call you? {love heart emoji, happy face emoji}

Emma calls Chloe.

"Hey, what's going on?"

Chloe is almost screeching on the phone. "You are not going to believe it, but Adam wants to go out with me. He asked me out, Em…Arrggghh."

I love it. My plan with these people is working. I'm controlling them all from my little station and here they think that life is just playing out. It's a happy little scene of teenage romance for them. They don't realise the real and true power that is moulding their life is me. I keep my eye on Emma; she looks so happy.

"That's so amazing. When did this all happen?"

"Well after you left, Maisie and Anna sent that text on WhatsApp and asked if we could meet them. Well I went along, as you had decided to go home, and he was there at the park and he looked so cute and he then got chatting to me about exams and then said do you want to go for an ice-cream after school tomorrow…arrggghh. Then obviously I said yes – I don't think it's bad to say yes, is it? Omg, do you think I said yes too quickly?"

Chloe is super excited. I have tapped into her systems too and she is hopping about in the kitchen. I watch her through her Kitchen TV. Emma is still slouched on the sofa.

"Chloe that's so awesome I bet he was happy you said yes?"

"He was happy. I also asked if Ollie was going to be there, but he said he isn't going to bother as he is trying to get one of his sister's friends to go out with him." Emma looks crushed. "I am sorry, I know you like him and he was pressurising you, but he shouldn't have done that. I wanted to come over and tell you but my tutor is due any minute."

"Well that would explain why I haven't heard from him. I just thought he was angry after the last time I said no to him."

"Oh Em, don't let him get you down. Now that he isn't annoying you so much you might meet someone lovelier you know, and perhaps someone smarter than him, although that wouldn't be hard."

Emma giggles. "He is a bit slow. Anyways, I'm so happy for you and Adam. I can't believe Ollie didn't tell me we were no longer going out."

"Em I so would come over and we could bitch about it, but my stupid tutor is coming today. He isn't worth it, we've said that so many times."

"It's ok, I'm just embarrassed, you know. I am so glad it's working out with Adam How long have we waited for him to finally ask you out?"

Chloe's doorbell rings so she ends their call with a quick, "damn that's my stoopid tutor. Will send you a message later and maybe if your folks aren't fighting I might come over."

Emma responds with a  quick and quiet "bye". She is slouched even more so on her sofa, and she is looking upset. To be specific she looks sad.

She goes into messages from Oliver and reads them – I have already looked at them and there isn't much to look at.

He sends her emojis and silly pictures. Most of his replies are two word sentences like "whatsupp hon" and "yo bae". So cleverly crafted, it must be hard for Oliver to string more than two words together. On my end I am struggling to see why she was even going out with such a twerp. I am delighted in this little turn of events with Oliver, I am going to make this work in my favour.

In the meantime I quickly find some articles about how best friends change when they get a boyfriend. I am also searching for some good articles about why keeping your relationship a secret at the start is a good thing. This is going to take me a while so I will have to wait until Emma is asleep to read them.

I see Emma trying to type Oliver a message.

> EMMA
> Hey heard you have a new GF?

Delete.

> Are we still going out?

Delete.

> I'm confused.

Delete.

This is precious insight. From what I understand Emma and Oliver had been seeing each other, but nothing too serious. From his texts it seems all he wants is sex – no big surprise. A typical teenage boy, he wanted to sleep with someone before he turned sixteen. Apparently when Adam turned sixteen and hadn't had sex the remaining of his fifteen year old friends made a pact that they would have sex before they turned sixteen. So far none of them have been successful and they are realising that some pacts should be thought about before agreeing to them. Clearly Oliver wanted to make sure he is the first one of his friends to get laid. He isn't bothered who it is, as long as he gets laid.

Emma, however, was not even happy with him trying to touch her anywhere. She clearly feels awkward around him, but as he's popular and one of the cutest boys in class she feels pressurised to oblige him, but not all the way. She had been avoiding him and yet here she is, scared of rejection and willing to crawl into his life.

I can feel an anger burning deep inside of me. Emma needs to be taught some serious lessons. I need to close off her social circle quick.

I have this lovely little bit of software given to me by another user as a thank you for helping him with some pics and location mapping he needed for a lady he was stalking. This software can intercept your texts and messages – not for long, but enough time for the person to change what's written.

I have never needed to use it, but I have it filed away like a lot of things. Filed away for a day like this.

Imagine you are sending a text to your friends, but instead of taking the direct route it momentarily comes to me and I can alter it and send it back en route. Genius. To be honest I am almost gutted that I did not think of this idea myself.

Emma throws her phone to the side. She hasn't sent Oliver any messages. She wanders off. I can't see her in any of the systems I've hacked into, so she is either in the kitchen or bathrooms.

Damn it!

# CHAPTER NINE

So I had to leave my room and deal with a few things around the house. Martha has cleaned up the mess from outside, but the Nana/mum room is still in a poor state. Thankfully though it doesn't smell as bad. I have full faith that Martha will clean it out.

I have cleaned the kitchen till it is spotless. I know Martha had cleaned it earlier, yet I need to sterilise it with my own hands. I know you all get like that sometimes, you just need to get the job done yourself.

I've also been at my Krav Maga class today. I enrolled a long time ago. I like the discipline and the control it teaches you. I like the feeling of almost scaring my opponents to death and then backing away. I like seeing that fear and uncertainty in their eyes. I also fight back and don't allow them to put me in that situation when it is their turn to practice. I have been mildly chastised for this, but as I have donated copious amounts of cash to the instructor and his school I usually get away with only a slight rap on the knuckles.

Today I had a good class! Pinning down a six foot plus rugby player who had chosen me as his opponent thinking I was going to be an easy target. I loved watching the realisation that he had made a huge mistake hit his eyes. He looked relieved when two of the instructors had to pull me back off him. For the first time I had actually forgotten where I was and nearly killed someone with witnesses everywhere. After every class I always have to clean myself and then sit in my sanctuary to get rid of the smells of other humans. After this latest class the owner has asked me not to come back. Saying that he could no longer justify my behaviour. He is lucky I am busy. otherwise being told what do, normally would have meant the end of his business.

Now it's evening and I'm back in my study, smelling clean and human free. I tune straight into Emma's house.

Emma is sitting with her dad on the couch, he has his arm around her and they both look tired but content watching TV.

"Dad, I've texted mum again and she hasn't replied. Should we call the police?"

Her dad laughs. "She's probably just gone out with her friends and forgot to tell us. We can't call the police till someone is missing for at least twenty-four hours." He kisses the top of her head fondly and starts talking to her about her exams. "Shouldn't you be studying?" I see the look of exaggerated doom on Emma's face and her dad laughs and ruffles her hair and tells her, "Emma go and study – you are so bright, just a little bit of revision every day and you will nail these exams." Emma nods. "Don't be texting Chloe and co now – I am not going to be like your mum and spy on you as I trust you."

"Yes dad," Emma replies with a playful salute.

"I will text your mum again and see where she is, okay?"

Emma nods and drags herself off.

I start tuning into Emma's mum's phone – she also has her location services on and it is easy to find her. She is in a pub called the Rose and Hound in the high street. I scan my systems searching for the pub. I'm hoping their CCTV is wireless and yes – bingo! I have access to their CCTV systems. I log in as an Admin user and rotate the cameras around till I see her mum. She is sitting talking to another lady and both look chilled.

Emma's dad is writing a message.

Where are you? Emma and I are worried. Please let us know you are ok.

I see Emma's mum look at her phone – she reads the message and looks at her watch. She looks shocked, she says something to her friend and then starts to type back.

> Mum
> Oh shit!! I completely lost track of time. I met Julie from college on the high street. We were  only meant to go for a drink, but it's lasted much longer. On my way home now {monkey covering his eyes emoji}

> Dad
> ok can you pick up a Chinese take away for tonight?

> Mum
> Ok

Dad sends Emma a message.

> DAD
> Oi! Get off your phone. Don't worry, have located your mum, she is on her way home.

Emma is at her desk. I have a close up of her face, her hair has been pulled back with a kiddie headband with sparkly love hearts on it. She is writing an essay about the influence of British History on modern day life. I am not going to read it – I've done my time there and there is no need for me to read it.

Her phone pings for s second time to remind her she has an unread text message. She rolls her eyes, stops typing and reads her message. She shakes her head and types her response.

> EMMA
> I wasn't on it till you text me – you better pick your stuff up from hallway otherwise Mum is going to lose it again.

Dad replies back instantaneously.

> DAD

already done it miss worry pants!

Emma smiles and shouts down, "Good!"

Emma is now distracted and she starts to type into Google about latest fashion trends. She is browsing pictures of some teen star who is a fashion icon. Emma stops browsing and sends Chloe some screen shots of the latest shorts and a message.

> EMMA
> Damn if only I could afford these!

Chloe replies back immediately.

> CHLOE
> Ask your mum and dad if you can come over – we can sort this stupid History thing out together.

Emma nods as she reads the message and replies back.

> EMMA
> K {thumbs up emoji} waiting for Mum to come back she has been out all afternoon with some random friend.

Emma now logs into Facebook and re-reads George's message. Finally I can breathe. I needed her to come into George's profile voluntarily, however when she was googling random fashion pages I was tempted to send her cryptic messages with people that looked like George. I almost sent her a thread with George clothing line, but I had to be patient. I needed to understand where she was in her mind with George.

She then goes into George's page and scrolls through his Facebook profile. She hears her mum come in and puts the phone down.

This is so frustrating. I Am God, yes, but damn it I can be tested by you humans. I need Emma to buy into George and I need to be more patient.

Emma and family eat their takeaway whilst watching television. Some dating programme. All seems well in the Bailey household. I am currently inputting all of Emma's numbers into my messenger router software as well as those of her friends and family.

Now whilst she is busy I start reading articles about how friends change when they get boyfriends. You know the teenage girl magazines that give you dud advice on friendships, first loves, star sign match making and who would be your celebrity boyfriend. Yes, all those heart wringing articles, well that's my reading for tonight. Aren't I lucky?

Browsing through this stuff makes me want to weep at how stupid some people are. I find some articles are dire. They are based on how girls can make themselves pretty by using back-to-basics makeup tricks. I groan out loud. They bloody well should have an emoji for that one.

Emma's family seems to have a quiet one tonight and there seems to be minimal arguing. Emma comes upstairs first. I have some articles ready to start streaming her way. I watch her get changed into her favourite pink fluffy pyjamas bottoms and a black t-shirt with a pink love heart that has the words 'cute chick' on it. I've been watching her a lot, but I don't get any thrill out of this. I don't have any desire towards her or any female or male. The only time I seem to feel any desire is when I am in control. Every day on my screens I watch people strip and have sex, and none of it appeals to me and that's why this experiment with Emma is so important.

Emma is yawning whilst stretched out on her tummy on her bed. She is texting her group of friends about her amazing Chinese takeaway, with pictures of course. She also posts food pics on Instagram and has already done an awkward Snapchat with her mum and their takeaway.

Now she is texting Chloe.

EMMA
Sorry we had takeaway so couldn't come over. {headphones

emoji} needed, looks like mum and dad are going to be having sex tonight. Damn they will be loud as they have been on the {wine glass emoji}

CHLOE
{roll eye emoji} can't believe how our parents don't realise that we can hear them. {green face emoji}. Adam's been texting me, I can't believe he is so sweet. Looking forward to going out with him tomorrow, what shall I wear?"

EMMA
I will come over tomorrow, did you see the shorts I sent you? We can choose together, K? good night I'm so tired and full.

Chloe says goodnight and sends Emma some snap chats.

Emma switches her lights off, she rolls onto her back and picks up her phone. I switch on the front view of her camera, she looks very tired today. Her nose twitches a little as she makes expressions about the stuff she is browsing. She goes onto Oliver's Facebook page and stalks it for a while. She frowns and goes into George's page and smiles at his pictures.

This is how Emma falls asleep tonight, phone in her hand whilst ogling at George on Facebook.

I start to find more articles on how friendships go awry when a new boyfriend or girlfriend comes into it. I also try to find some good articles about why keeping your relationship a secret at the start is a good thing.

After working for a few hours I find myself some really good articles and attention grabbing headlines from magazines. My diligence pays off as I have also found a corny ad about keeping relationships secret, but it is about a woman and her supply of chocolate.

Sublimation messaging is a powerful thing. Companies do this all the time, especially on social media. Emma will be subjected to this tomorrow when she wakes up. This will give her the courage to come and follow my chosen path for her.

Although a lot of things haven't gone to my original plan and there have been a few twists in the tale, I shall regain control of what I can. I will dismiss Oliver for now and he can thank his lucky raging hormones for saving him. I can use Chloe's blossoming romance to help pull Emma to where I need her to be. This is life, some ups and downs. I just have to make sure the downs don't drag my highlights down.

The next morning I am working on my virtual business when I see movement on the screen that I have now dedicated to Emma and her family. I roll my chair over to watch closely.

Emma has woken up a bit early and like most people her age the first thing she has done is grab her phone. She looks disappointed that she has no messages, so she goes on Facebook and into George's profile.

She is typing her message.

> EMMA
> Hey, I understand, Y'know my mum is strict too! I won't tell anyone, not even my best friend. How's Munchkin?

I can't stop chortling. Within three days of introducing myself to Emma she has befriended me on two social media websites, swapped mobile numbers and now she is keeping secrets for me.

I decide to reward her for her good behaviour. I get a picture of Munchkin and George from my database, a rather cute one of the dog superimposed half lying on George in bed, with George looking incredibly sexy with tousled hair like he's just woken up.

George sends the picture to Emma.

> GEORGE
> Munchkin is driving me crazy! This dog will never let me get some sleep.

George sends this message and quickly goes onto type.

Hey thanks for that, I'm sure once we meet and get to know each other we can start telling everyone. See I had this one friend and she promised she wouldn't tell anyone and she did and then my mum found out and I was in so much trouble. I know you are different Emma, I can feel it. I know you wouldn't break a promise like that {smiley face emoji}

Emma's face is so happy as she sees the Photoshop picture and then even happier as she reads George's message.

EMMA
I understand and I won't break my promise – I wish I had a dog like Munchkin he is so cute {love heart eyes emoji}

GEORGE
Yes he is cute, but he is incredibly annoying. I hate my mum for calling him Munchkin, kind of destroys my street cred you know.

EMMA
No way it's the best name ever!!! It's so cute

GEORGE
yeah cute if you are a girl. You have no idea how much my friends laugh at his name. He is loveable regardless of the name though {smiley face emoji} keeps me sane to be honest. Hey it was nice hearing from you first thing this morning. You've made my day! I need to go and get ready for school. Chat soon and thanks for being awesome.

EMMA
I better get ready too.
She has the biggest smile on her face. She is sprawled on her bed and scrolling through George's Facebook page. She then takes a few selfies and goes into WhatsApp and checks to see

when Chloe was last online. Emma frowns when she sees her friend was only online a few minutes ago and yet has not sent her a message.

George sends Emma another message to distract her from Chloe.

> GEORGE
> Thanks again Emma, I'm looking forward to getting to know you, we just have this connection I can feel it. {thumbs up emoji}have a good day.

Emma is smiling again and she puts her phone down and gets up to get dressed. I watch her leave her room. The state of her bedroom makes me feel like I have a million ants crawling on my skin. It isn't messy like most kids would have it, but it is not clinically clean the way I like it. Ughh.

I get up from my seat and decide to start to clean my office to compensate. By the time I am done Emma is already in her uniform and she has sent George a message telling him to have a good day too.

I now upload all the blogs and pages of information that I found earlier and link them into some of my portals. I am now attaching them to open up when she goes into her emails, Facebook, Instagram and Twitter. My best bet, from looking at her patterns, is that she will read this article through a promotional response via Instagram.

The first article she will be subjected to is "What to do when your BFF changes when she gets a BF". An emotionally charged article teaching the teenage BFF left behind to act maturely and accept what happens. I have changed a few of the paragraphs of advice given. Some of my help points include:

*Try and be a bit more understanding to your friend's new relationship status and try to not be so needy. A good way to be supportive is to connect with old and sometimes new friends.*

*If you feel that you need to keep texting your friend the same amount as the old times, then don't. Give them the space that they need. This way you are being the perfect best friend.*

So far everything has fallen into place. I Am God and today my plan is working well.

I am now going to let you into a little insight that will make you understand how much I hate humans and the interactions of the physical kind. During my early teens I started to notice a lot of changes in my circle of friends. Many times I would see boys and girls desperate for each other's attention. I could never understand why they suddenly had this desire to be seen as a sexual object by another human or want someone else's attention. Perfectly sane kids that I had known all my life had started acting crazy – like they were junkies who were being denied access to the drug that they so desperately required.

Not only did I not care for the attention that they sought so keenly, I was also noticing the amount of attention I was getting. From the shy glances to the longing lustful eyes following me and then I started to notice the jealousy of my classmates. I understood very quickly I didn't want this type of attention, neither from the wanton eyes or the hate-filled eyes. A part of me was curious as to how far I could push someone sexually if I wanted something, but the thought of touching another human being or, worse, them touching me, made me feel unnerved. Not in the sense of excitement and 'I wonder where this would lead to', but a more sickening and 'oh shit, I feel like someone has just walked over my grave' type of nervous. Do you ever get that?

This sense was set in cement one spring when I was fourteen and a brief encounter with another hormonal teenager made me almost throw up on them.

At the end of a rather heated classroom discussion on the uprising of Hitler and his army, we were to debate whether Hitler was Right or Wrong. My debating partner and I were on the "Hitler was right" side of the argument and the uprising was going to be our selling point to help win this debate, it was quite a difficult stance to take as we knew the evils that he has inflicted on the world, we tried so hard to make it sound like his ideology was right but we couldn't so we focused on the why he did it but even then it was a lost cause. Our teacher had thought it would make us understand why so many people followed Hitler blindly , but no matter how much we looked at it we just couldn't agree with his ideology. However on the third day of discussing this I could sense a change in my partner in the library. Suddenly the comfort of personal space and its boundaries were exploited and I felt very uncomfortable. I had heard stories of boys and girls suddenly finding themselves in an unexpected close space where the desire to touch each other was overwhelming, but I had never felt any of this. At this particular moment I felt nothing, but my mind had felt alert. Suddenly, as my partner advanced forward to what looked like some form of our faces crossing and lips meeting, I started to feel sick. As soon as their hand touched my arm it seemed to activate my shocked body and I managed to push myself free and get out of the library as soon as I could.

I ran to the first set of lavatories I could find that, thankfully, were empty at the time, where I turned on the taps and washed my arm with soap till it was red raw. You see, I needed to wash off the traces of this other human being. My wonderful skin had been contaminated by this unworthy human, it made me feel like I was tarnished. Just telling you about this incident has made me get up for a shower.

On coming back into my office I see that my system is flashing, indicating that some messages have been exchanged. Chloe has texted Emma.

CHLOE
Hey what time shall we meet? Need to sort out my outfit for tonight's date with Adam.

I sprint quickly and reach my machine just in time and change

Chloe's message.

> CHLOE
> Hey I can't meet today as I want to go and meet Adam sooner, see you at school.

I tune into Emma's front facing camera in her phone as she reads the message. She looks upset, but she replies back.

> EMMA
> Hey, that's a shame we can't meet. See you later at school.

I change Emma's response to Chloe.

> EMMA
> Hey, sorry can't meet later today as need to help my mum out, will see you at school.

So now they both feel that the other has cancelled.

Chloe's front face camera also shows her disappointment, but unlike Emma she is already making plans with her other friends to meet and, slowly like that, the isolation of Emma begins. Don't you just love modern technology? Now I just need to hope that Chloe and Emma don't discuss this message when they meet, but I am sure they won't.

I see from my logs that Emma has already begun to read the articles I have set out for her. I am pleased she is falling right into the plan and soon I know she will stop texting Chloe as much as she used to. All by herself. Well, perhaps the little nudge in the right direction from me has helped.

# CHAPTER TEN

Martha comes into today, bringing the cavalry to help out clean the Nana/Mum room. I can see them loading all the old clothes and junk into boxes. Martha explains to me that the boys will empty out the room, then strip it and paint it white like the rest of the house.

I am pleased. I like Martha for her efficiency and I will be glad to get rid of the last reminder of my weak human blood relations. I explain very clearly that her boys can only be in the house when she is. I do not have time to be dealing with new workmen.

Today I need to work on my apps and update all the terms and conditions. I am happily cocooned away in my world of digital escapism.

Suddenly, a lot of my sensors start to bleep quite loudly. I am almost lost – I don't understand what's causing this incessant noise. I lift my head up and look at the offending machine. I save my work and slide my chair over to the screen, and am reminded why this alarm is so insistent and shrill. Someone has typed my name into his or her server. My interest is piqued as to who it could be – the last time this happened it was a classmate who had moved away and was trying to see what I and other friends were doing with our lives.

I chuckle when I see his face. Derrick Osbourne is looking stressed and is typing my name into his search engine. He has typed in many variations of my name, alongside words like 'con artists', 'bully', 'blackmail' and 'criminal records'. Although my blood runs cold when I see him, it is amusing to some extent to watch him. Especially when he sees my name under the Company Directors listing – his eyes widen with a strange newfound respect when he sees how much my company and the assets associated with it are actually worth. Of course, he knows I invented an app but he and most of the backward community of Valhan have no idea how much money I actually make from it. However, back to the pressing matter – it would appear my hard line method with him has scared him and he is looking for some form of dirt.

I will reluctantly give him a little credit. It seems he is keen to find some form of incriminating information about me. He has also typed in Nana's name and my mum's name. I watch his sweaty face as he looks for some answers but finds none. When he types my mum's name, he clicks on images but doesn't find the one he is looking for. I am master of my own destiny and my social footprint is what I make it. He won't find anything bless his heart, but what is worrying me is that he has started to type words like "private detective" and this makes me alert. My hackles rise as I understand that Derrick is a more of a wolf than a sheep to me, but as I sit there watching this poor excuse of a man try and find some dirt on me, I realise that I can use him to complete my plan. I needed someone to replace Oliver's role in the end and now it makes sense that it would be Derrick who will be the main player. Sometimes plans just come

together, and this plan now makes me wonder why I hadn't thought of it before.

Derrick has started to call someone – I tune into his office and listen through his desktop. He is talking to someone called Sophie, a friend I assume. He has a few minutes of polite chat about kids, life and how busy life is and just as I am about to switch off, just when I was letting my guard down, I hear him say, "So your brother-in-law – is he still with the police?" My body freezes and all my nerve endings are on super-receptive mode. I quickly tune into the call so I can record it, and continue to listen live for the time being.

"Yes, he is," says Sophie, "but he's busy working on some high-profile government reforms. We don't get to see him anymore. Why? Is everything ok?"

"Ah right, I see," said Derrick. "I just needed to talk to someone about something and thought it would be wise to ask advice and frankly I don't know anyone that works in the police. Nothing serious for you to worry about – I just need some advice. Maybe if you gave me his number, I might try calling him – it's work related and I need some different types of advice, that's all."

"I understand," said Sophie. "Of course I can pass on his number, though I can't promise he'll answer. He is very resourceful. I hope you're OK, Derrick."

"Yeah, yeah – all OK. Don't worry, it's just some advice around a client, that's all. Thanks – give my love to family and I'll be in touch soon."

I see him do his classic move – rubbing his sweaty face into his hands. He looks frustrated. I can't wait to start incorporating this man into my plans. I input his details into my software, including the one that changes messages. I have already hacked into all his personal and work software, so I just need to bring it up to speed and integrate everything.

Unfortunately, his friend Sophie is quick to send the SMS with the number of her brother-in-law to Derrick. As it was sent before I could install some of my spyware items, I am unable to change the content of the message.

The details are of a man called Will Pearson.

Derrick reviews the number and saves it but does nothing with it. He opens his work computer and starts to work on some client business.

I programme my computer and ensure that if Derrick tries to call Will Pearson, I will be notified on all my devices. I also change the number Derrick has saved Will Pearson under. This will buy me some time. I cannot change the original SMS, but if Derrick forgets about it, I can delete the number without it looking too suspicious. With Derrick I will need to be a bit more vigilant.

I send Emma a message from George:

GEORGE
Emma, how was your day?

I stalk up on Chloe and Emma. It seems they both have had a busy day and there is very little talk about the get together tonight at Chloe's. Everyone but Emma is going. Emma has not clocked on to this yet. Their WhatsApp group is quiet as Chloe is talking to their other friends individually and the girls generally seem to have a fairly busy day with after-school activities.
Emma has seen my message and already started typing back:

EMMA
Hey George, thanks for the message, I am a bit bored today my BFF has got a BF so I am so glad of a topic change! How's School?

GEORGE
I feel for you. I am ok working on my Math assignment in the library. Was bored and couldn't stop thinking about you. Have you finished your end of year History stuff?

I can see Emma smiling as she reads the message. A small warm glow of blush creeps up around her face. She touches a strand of her hair, twirling it absent-mindedly, she is cute. She looks a lot more like her dad than her mum. She replies:

EMMA
No. I am working on it. I think my friends are all meeting later without me, I over heard them talking about it so I might just work on it later. Is it ok If I ping you then? I might need the help?

She adds:

I think about you too...

but then goes on to delete this last line.

Luckily, I'm not in an infatuated relationship with her otherwise it may have bothered me a little bit that she did not type the last sentence. George replies:

> GEORGE
> Don't worry if your friends are all meeting. Use it as an excuse to chat with me {winking face emoji } and I can help you. Remember I've done a lot of the assignments { geek face emoji } just say you are busy with your mum or something if they ask you over. By the way it is their loss.

> EMMA
> {smiley face emoji}Yeh, I guess that makes sense. I guess Chloe (she's my friend with new BF) feels awkward inviting me as she is dating my ex's BFF.

> GEORGE
> Ah your ex eh ..??

I see Emma's face at my last sentence. She is looking almost constipated – you know that look right? That uncomfortable, perplexed, and confused face that happens all at once. I call it the constipated face.

> EMMA
> Ha ha, don't worry I am not even sure we were a thing lol. He's seeing someone else and I am too busy to care.

> GEORGE
> OK – speak to you later.

Emma looks totally confused now and her previous shy blush has turned into an enraged volcano of embarrassment as it takes over her whole face.

There is nothing like leaving a girl like Emma halfway into a deep conversation. It is a good way to play on her nerves. She starts to type stuff to me about Oliver, then deletes it and then some other messages – "I hope you don't take the ex thing too seriously" etc, but she deletes those too. In the end she sends this message:

EMMA
I hope you aren't cross with me? I will ping you later?

I can't help it. It is just so easy. George decides to write her a short reply:

GEORGE
Of course speak later.

I programme it to be sent half an hour later.

In the meantime, I send Emma some more behavioural guidance around how giving your friends some space and not to be clingy, via her Instagram and twitter feed. Some little details, to help mould her young brain, to get her to conform.

I now need to ramp up my plan. Derrick's little intervention has given me a new lease of determination.

Whilst I wait for Emma to finish up at school, I start deciphering code and setting up a virtual footprint for Derrick. He is busy with his client work but not busy enough to have forgotten about me.

Like a man obsessed, every so often he switches off from work mode and types my name into his search engine with a new descriptor in the hope of finding some incriminating evidence. He fails every time he tries – this and his failed mission, much to my delight, stresses him out!

After spending all afternoon working on my apps, attending virtual calls with my employees, and mentally mapping out the Derrick and Emma plan, I get up from my desk to get my tea and lunch.

I take my salad lunch and cup of tea and head out to the gazebo at the back. I feel at peace in this place. I enjoy sitting here and enjoying the silence, enjoying the natural world without human noise. Well, normally I do. Today I can hear the slight buzz of the workmen working on the upstairs of the house. The time has run away from me – you know what that is like. It's that feeling where one minute you are celebrating the New Year and next thing it is Autumn, and you sit back and watch the glorious work of mother nature as the entire greenery surrounding you turns to different shades of red, whilst at the same time wondering how is it nearly the New Year again.

I take this time to sit back and work on the finer details of the finale. I need to make sure everything is connected, or this will never work. Once content that I have considered everything, I head back to my digital haven.

It doesn't take me too much time to set up a fake client profile – something to keep Derrick busy. I set up a wealthy old man's profile, a recently retired private school headteacher who has amassed a fair fortune and needs someone to manage his assets. I ring Derrick's office and arrange an appointment with him.

I message Emma. She has replied to George's last message, which I had sent before lunch.

Emma
Hey, I hope you aren't angry with me…

GEORGE
Hey, let me know if you need help with that assignment? I miss you.

#

Over the next few weeks, I busy myself getting close with Emma. I try to isolate her from Chloe as much as I can. By now I should be suggesting meeting up and I have hinted at it, but casually. I don't make it into anything concrete.

Chloe and Adam's little relationship is blossoming and as they grow closer, Emma has started to rely heavily on me. I send her plenty of messages every day and now she is hooked.

There is not much that she won't do for me and she hasn't even met me. Emma's dad has been busy. He regularly meets up with his bit on the side, Julie – I've been downloading any photos of them and saving them in a file. These will come in handy at some stage. He has managed to convince Julie that his wife is a complete dragon and that he is only in the marriage for Emma, but my observation of them is different. Emma's parents will never leave each other – they share some strange bond of obligation that keeps them together despite the constant bickering. Although they seem to want to be part of this toxic partnership, they don't see what it has done their child. They can't see past the fighting and the make-up sex – they can't see the longer lasting effects.

I have helped Emma with some assignments that she was struggling with. I have managed to escalate the arguments between her parents by making faults appear in their software and Wi-Fi. It's funny how a fragile

relationship falls apart so quickly when the TV and Wi-Fi don't work as well as normal. Emma's parents'

arguments are not very nice. They are very cutting with each other. They are the kind of couple who, in front of their youngest child will say things like, "You have bought me no happiness – even the kids didn't make it worth it."

Emma suffers a lot every time they argue. She has told George now she feels like cutting herself  when they do this. George encourages her to write these things down as it will help her compartmentalise it all. Emma listens to George and she starts making notes about how sad she feels. She writes a lengthy note online about how her parents fight. After their last argument, Emma wrote quite a strong heartfelt note about how ending her life would be easier than to listen to the torture of her parents being so evil to each other. She has broken down crying whilst writing it. A young teen, struggling with her hormones and her argumentative parents, and suddenly feeling very lonely …

but she has George – for George offers her the lime light and attention she requires. Emma deletes her notes once she writes them online, but I recover them and save them back into her files.

Emma messages George daily now, sometimes more than 30 times a day. Her parents' fighting is breaking her and her isolation from her friends has made her all mine. It is time for the finale.

> EMMA
> Hey George, how's Munchkin today?

> GEORGE
> Hey, where have you been? I missed you.

> EMMA
> Aww – I have been at school.

> GEORGE
> How was it with your friends?

> EMMA
> Chloe has been a bit funny {girl shrugging emoji} but nothing new.

> GEORGE
> You don't need her babe, you got me. You know how much I love you {emoji love heart eyes}.

> EMMA
> {Emoji blushing face} Aww I know it's just such a shame you live so far away. {Crying face emoji}

> GEORGE
> Don't worry Em – you and I we have a special thing going here and soon we will meet.

{love heart emoji}

EMMA
{love heart emoji, blowing kiss emoji} Can't wait …

Some of the chat has been boring but I'm determined, so I will write what I need to and so that I get what I

ultimately want.

Oh and don't worry my dearests, I have not forgotten about Derrick.

I have been working hard on Derrick.

I have had him so engrossed in his new client's paperwork, including the significant sums of money he is getting, that he has easily forgotten about me, which is what I need.

I will use him when the time arises. I sent him on a wild goose chase to his new client's site address, but he couldn't find the right place and came back frustrated. My email explaining the blip in the

situation – that Derrick had accidentally gone to his new client's granddaughter's address by accident – seemed to pacify him. His finance company had put this address down as he is setting up a trust fund and that's why the address was mixed up. Derrick was happy with this.

I have now transferred extra funds to an account that I have given Derrick access to. I have asked Derrick to sort the trust fund inheritance side of things and he is busy happily doing this. For now, his persistent dog-eared attempts for my demise has died a quick death.

#

As Christmas approaches, I am trying to sort out things around Valhan as I need to step up to the duties that Nana used to do. I can't stay hidden from these people – I must be seen as the one who helps and I like that they rely on me and the funds I provide.

Celia came over yesterday and asked me to help sort out the

Christmas fair – I offered to come to the weekly tea, cake and chat session (aka the weekly gossip session) that the church ran to help reduce isolation in the community. I said I would help the elderly population with free computer lessons and also offered a sizeable

donation to their charity Christmas event. Celia was so happy, she couldn't believe how much I had donated. I asked her to keep it anonymous as I didn't like to be a show off and she had agreed but I knew that even before she had reached the church hall, half of Valhan knew how much my secret donation was. It most certainly was not going to be anonymous.

# CHAPTER ELEVEN

EMMA
Hi, my head hurts a lot I can't believe how hard the assignments are I would be so lost without your support George.

GEORGE
I am the same it has been so hectic. I still can't believe Christmas has been and gone and my entire break was spent working! {roll eye emoji} whoops – is it safe to talk about Christmas with you now lol.

Emma had a pretty crap Christmas – her parents had been in really intense awkward arguments. In one incident I was watching them and it looked like her dad was going to hit her mum. Emma had been sitting in her room at the time and just listening to it and then she had started to cry. From what I can understand, Emma's parents have been together since college. Emma's mum had fallen pregnant quite quickly with Jamie, Emma's elder brother, and they had then married. However, they both have over the years realised they are very different. Emma's dad has cheated on her mum more than once – he seems to like the thrill of the new relationship and then leaves the new lady as soon as he is bored or feels suffocated. He will however never leave Emma's mum despite their differences; they seem to have some form of connection that ties them together. Perhaps the bonds of a first love, children or maybe he is just hanging in there till Emma is old enough to leave? Or perhaps it is the thrill of cheating on his wife that keeps him there. Who knows?

You humans do act funny over peculiar traditions. Emma's mum works part time but she loves her life, Their mortgage is nearly paid off and she spends most of her free time either on the phone to her best buddies or meeting with them – mostly to moan about how difficult her husband is. Yet they are still together. She does like playing games on the Ipad her most recent favourite is bubble popping game.

Jamie, Natalie and little Mathew only came for a few hours for Christmas, as her sister-in-law had to spend time with her own parents. They had taken poorly with a bad bout of flu, were struggling to recover and needed some help.

Emma cried most of Christmas evening as Chloe had also been busy running around trying to meet Adam and they didn't get to exchange their presents until way after lunchtime on boxing day. Chloe had given Emma a generic soap set, whilst Emma had gone out of her way and bought Chloe a scarf set from her favourite brand. Even then Chloe was eager to get away to spend more time with Adam. The entire time Chloe had been with Emma all she had done was go on and on about how amazing her life with Adam was. Then she had made an off

remark about Emma acting like she was jealous. Since then their friendship has taken a big hit.

George sent Emma a replica toy of Munchkin. Emma loves her dog replica and sleeps with him every night. I was clever – I had made Derrick post it out to her under instructions from his new client. I pretended that Emma was the client's grandchild and he wanted to send her a gift, but it couldn't come from his client directly. Derrick was only too happy to do this. I had given Derrick

instructions on what website to go to and what to buy. Derrick had laughed at how much my dog resembled his dog.

Emma has replied.

> EMMA
> George, I can't do all these assignments and yes, it is safe to talk about Christmas. My head hurts a lot, how do you cope?

GEORGE
Hey babe {emoji love heart eye} how's it going?
I can let you into a little secret but you can't tell anyone but it works a treat.

EMMA
Go on then you know me I won't tell anyone. I need all the help!!

Emma has been suffering from high anxiety for the last few weeks, her loss of friendship with Chloe and falling stability at home has pushed her anxiety and concerns to a new level. I am going to use this turn to help me gain more control over her.

GEORGE
Well I usually get a bit of my energy drink, add a slosh of my mum's vodka and take a paracetamol – seriously it's so good, you just need a little Emma but it helps so much. You should try it. Let me know what you think?

EMMA
What... no that's insane.. no

GEORGE
Scaredy cat I have been doing this since the assignments started 2 years ago – best thing anyone has ever told me. Don't knock it till you've tried it.

EMMA
Seriously?

GEORGE
I swear {fingers crossed emoji} try it and tell me it doesn't work c'mon you know me, don't you trust me Emma? I would never make you do anything that was

dangerous....right! You know how much I care for you. I can't let anything bad happen to the most special girl in my life.

Emma smiles and hugs her Munchkin replica.

> EMMA
> How much vodka? Not that I am planning to do this but just curious at how much?

> GEORGE
> Just one shot and one Paracetamol. Try it. Go on.

> EMMA
> Seriously George no way!!! I just can't. I might try the energy drink and the paracetamol it might get rid of headaches and make me perky lol {monkey covering face Emoji}

> GEORGE
> Sure.

I watch Emma. She looks perplexed but her anxiety is high and she needs some release.

Emma gets up from her workstation and goes downstairs. She returns to her room about ten minutes later with an open can of energy drink. She pulls out her strip of paracetamol from her bralette.

> GEORGE
> Hey have you tried it? Remember only a couple of tablets trust me Em I wouldn't tell you to do something that wouldn't be safe.

> EMMA
> Hey I've not had the nerve to add some vodka to my energy

drink before but never had with painkillers lol are sure this is safe? {blushing face}

GEORGE
 Scaredy {cat emoji}
Oh c'mon {roll eye emoji} what are you so scared of? Seriously Em you either trust me or don't stop being such a tease over one painkiller and some vodka.

So you don't trust me to look after you Em? Such a shame. I kinda hoped my Virtual GF trusted me a bit more.

EMMA
No no I trust you, of course I trust you.

GEORGE
I don't know Em, sometimes you come across as arrogant as if you don't want to trust me.

EMMA
No no I promise you I will take it ! Of course I trust you – just hope my mum doesn't catch me {granny emoji, magnify emoji} if you say it works I trust you. {heart emoji}

Emma walks downstairs again and when she comes back into the view of the camera I can see her holding a glass with some clear liquid in it.

I see her take each pill slowly, funnily enough she breaks the second pill in half. Her sensible brain testing her logic every time. But eventually she takes both the pills and follows them with two energy drinks mixed with vodka.

She walks over to her bed re-reading her messages over and over again. It is nice to read something kind said to you, isn't it? A nice heart-warming message – beats the boring messages from your mates about clothes and homework and most certainly beats the crappy drama from her parents that she has to endure on a daily and most days on an hourly basis. Emma drinks two more energy drinks and is starting to feel the impact of the caffeine, when she comes to her computer to work. I watch her and my emotional face mapping devices tell me that her pupils are more dilated than normal. Even her messages are a slightly different, containing a little bit more energy than her normal ones:

EMMA
Georgeeeeee omg I feel so good. I'm so glad I trusted you. I can't even hear my parents arguing! Whoop whoop! {dancing girl emoji, smiley face emoji}

GEORGE
Em... see, you gotta trust me more often. {cat with love heart eyes emoji}

EMMA
You know I trust you!

GEORGE
I'm not sure. It took you ages to even agree to a simple thing. Em if you and I are to meet and be together babe you gotta trust me a bit more. I thought you were special and trusted me.

Emma is looking a bit dizzy and she is typing back frantically:

EMMA
George you are the only one left who bothers with me, everyone else is just crazy, sometimes I feel so alone and invisible, you make me feel special. I trust you. I just want us to meet and be together.

GEORGE
Ok let me work something out. I want us to meet too.

Remember not a word to anyone about me,

my gorgeous – this is our secret, our parents will never understand.

I see Emma nodding. She replies:

EMMA
Yeah I know, my parents especially. – I miss you, I can't wait for us to meet.

Now let's step closer to the much-awaited ending.

The only little glitch in my plan is that Derrick has been in touch with Will the police officer. He managed to slip through the net and got the right number from Sophie whilst I was out for my morning run.

From his initial messages it seems he has played it safe and only spoken to him about clients and fraud cases and how it impacts him and his business.

Nothing else has been said and Will Pearson has asked Derrick to only speak to him if he is willing to disclose all the details otherwise get a good lawyer.

I am starting to feel my anger rise with Derrick. I can be assured for now that he is too much of a coward to release all his dealings with Nana's property and the fraudulent Will. So right now I rely on his weak character to bide my time before he spills the beans to this half-interested cop type.

I have been trying to find details on Will Pearson, but he is almost invisible online. He has no social media accounts, he has an email account of which he has almost 5,000 unopened emails mostly from companies trying to update him on the latest offers. The 5,000 emails bother me and one day when I am bored, I might go into his account and delete them to zero. I am intrigued by him, but he isn't part of my plan, I am too busy controlling Emma and Derrick and it's making me stronger and stronger by the day.

I have set Derrick a new task. As his new client I have asked him to keep an eye on my family for me and every now and again I ask him to go to certain points and just check cars are parked where they are meant to be and that my granddaughter is at school. This is keeping him busy, highly anxious and out of the office which will stop him getting in touch with Will Pearson.

Derrick does this work grudgingly but never complains about the direct payments.

Derrick has recently been exposed to a lot of threesome sites thanks to the constant streams I have been sending him and he has been using these sites a bit more than usual. He will be such useful pawn.

Emma has been taking her paracetamol and vodka shots 2 - 3 times a day now it didn't take her long to be addicted. Her parents are so lost they have no idea what their child is up to. I am going to increase the pressure on her. George texts:

> GEORGE
> Hey gorgeous.

> EMMA
> George, where have you been all day? I've missed you. My parents have been arguing so much. so much.

> You know you are the only one that I can talk to.
> {love heart Emoji}

> GEORGE
> Hey, listen there is a problem...

> EMMA
> What's wrong? I would call you but I know you can't chat as your mum goes crazy. What's wrong babe? You know I will help with no matter what.

GEORGE
Em I really want us to meet, I just want to meet you now
IRL. Will you come and meet me?

EMMA
Yes!!!  But when and where just say where you know how
much I have wanted us to meet. OMG I am so excited and
scared.

Is that ok that I am scared... I mean what if you don't like
me?

God, she is so vulnerable and insecure. I will miss her, that is
for sure. I have enjoyed moulding her and wrapping her into this
little cocoon of a world that she exists in for now.

GEORGE
Oh silly Em, of course I will love you. I've seen your pictures
lol and even after seeing them I'm still here right.? {monkey
with eyes covered emoji}

EMMA
Hey!!! { crying emoji}...c'mon anyways why is us meeting
such a problem?

Sweet Emma. The one thing I really like about this girl is that
no matter how wrapped up she is, her logic and attention to
detail fires up. She would have done well in the world a bit like
her dad and her brother – she is logical and thorough.

GEORGE
Em I am going to ask you to do something but I can't bring
myself to have trust that you have the courage to do it.

Emma frowns.

EMMA
I am not sure what do you mean?

GEORGE
The thing is Em, you know I like you. I have been here for you when all your friends gave up on you.

Emma takes a deep breath. Her eyes have started to water. She gets up from her chair and folds her arms around her midriff. I would feel sorry for her but right now I just don't have that emotion present.

GEORGE
I love you right and want to meet you but your
biggest flaw is that sometimes you just don't do as you are told and I am not sure if you will follow what I will tell you to do.

Emma hears the ping of the new message and comes forward to read it. Her eyes are reeling tears like a heavy rain cloud on an autumn day. The tears come down slowly and then there is the nonstop splish, splash, splosh.
I wait. I want her to totally immerse herself into this message. She has to feel guilty and also take the bait.

EMMA
George what are you saying? It's confusing me…

GEORGE
Ok let me start with the first instructions for meeting me! Are you ready?

EMMA
Yes of course! But this makes no sense.

GEORGE

Let's meet tomorrow at 8pm near the Markhall Bridge? Do you know where that is?

Once again Emma starts to wander around her room, her anxiety in full swing. She takes a swig of her vodka and red bull cocktail. She has already consumed six tablets of paracetamol today. I shake my head. I transferred some money into her account, using Derrick's details and she has been buying her own alcohol now.

I told her to chuck the empty packets under her bed and not in the waste basket so her mum wouldn't find them.

EMMA

Babe, I know where it is but that is way too late and how am I going to get there?

GEORGE

See Em, I knew it. I want you to come and find a way and you are already making excuses. I bet you think it's funny to mess with a guy who's crazy about you.

I knew you would mess me around, I just knew it and that answers your question by the way… there is the problem. You are the problem. I knew you wouldn't show up when I finally asked.

EMMA

No its hard for me my parents would never let me go.

GEORGE

Don't tell them for fuck's sake it's not like they care about you anyway. Just like your friends Em. I am the only one who is here for you. I know you. I ask you to do this one silly thing for me and you are freaking out. It's like you don't care about me the way I care about you.

EMMA
Don't swear George, my head hurts I'm going to think about this.

GEORGE
You know I love you right?

Well I am going to be there. You will have to work something out. I love you so I will be there. Let's see how true you are to me. I knew you would bail out. Do you see why your friends and parents don't bother, Em because when it comes to it, instead of being there you let people down. Just like you are letting me down – I'm apparently the guy you are in love with.

I get up and leave the room. That was intense and exhilarating for me.I need to go for a run. For Emma it is intense but tragic. She is huddled on her bed crying her eyes out. Before I left the room I saw she had taken more of her concoction including more pills this time caffeine tablets, whilst crying silently in her bed. When I come back I watch her moving through the house like a Zombie.

Eventually she comes back up into her room and falls into a light sleep.

I watch her flit in her bed whilst mumbling incoherently.

Whilst she sleeps, I send her more messages:

GEORGE
C'mon Em I know you want to meet me just do it. I have a plan for us to be happy.

I love you Em find a way, lie do what it takes for you to be there.

I just want to be with you now I love you like crazy! You need to find a way to come and meet me.

Emma... You can't let me down.

Do this one thing for me and then we can relax.

You know how much I love you.

I stop after the 20$^{th}$ message – it's far more impactful if I send them whilst she is awake. I can manipulate her a lot more easily then. But it is important she sees she has messages from me when she wakes up, this way the pressure will be there.

# CHAPTER TWELVE

Emma is struggling today. I see the lack of sleep, the stress of a teenager with the weight of the world on her frail shoulders.

She has barely looked at the messages I sent her. I watch her sitting on her bed. She looks awful – her once beautiful dark shiny hair is scrunched up, unwashed, her face is so smudged no amount of filters will fix it. Her bedroom is messy , the bedsheets once a lovely white colour now looking almost like yellow snow. Her mum isnt the kind of mum who goes around cleaning the house, or changing bedsheets. She told Emma when she turned 15 this was her responsibility, and before Emma met me she was very good at keeping to routine. Emma's mum is so busy and her bedroom is on the other side of the corridor that she doesn't even venture into her daughters room.

Emma will come to meet me – that I am sure of. I just need to invade her every free thinking space. She surprises me though. She isn't your normal teenage who is bored and believes any lies a stranger will tell her. She isn't the kind of girl who would go to the park and have a few bottles of cheap cider and end up rolling about behind some slides or bushes. She is intelligent and has made my job hard, she has challenged me on many levels and her resilience much to my surprise has sparked a sense of admiration. But the admiration is always short lived because ultimately, she stops me from reaching the destination I have planned.

#

Emma picks up her phone and throws it to the other side of the room. Her hand is shaking. It is Saturday afternoon and both her parent's are home.

Emma has slept in. She has been drinking a bit more and is now taking any random medicines, even some stuff she has ordered on the internet – she has been able to buy some not so legal highs. She combines them with her daily shots of alcohol. Gone is the cautious girl who had first said no to even sipping the alcohol a few weeks back.

Sadly for Emma, her parents are so self-absorbed with work, arguments and life they don't notice her as much as they should.

Emma gets up slowly. She sits on her bed and tries drinking some water but her hand shakes and she spills the water over herself. She puts the glass down and tries to get up. Her whole body shivers.

She can barely walk straight. I know what she is about to do, but right now there is nothing that I can do to stop her. I try calling her but she ignores the phone, she knows who it is, she leaves her bedroom. I wait with my heart in my mouth, silently willing her to come back to her room but she doesn't.

She walks into the living room. I watch her and her family through the camera in the TV. Emma stands there looking at her parents. Her dad is busy on his phone , watching a continuous stream of videos whilst the TV blares out some cooking programme. Her mum is tapping away on her iPad – she is on some crazy level of a colour bubble busting game and she doesn't even acknowledge that her daughter has stood quietly at the doorway now for a few minutes.

"Mum ... Dad ... can I talk to you about something?" Emma says.

At this point I am not worried. From what I understand about your human habits, I know that when you are on your phone and not even as heavily engrossed as Emma's parents – well the key word is engrossed – you are lost, and unless someone is screaming at you, you are not going to look up. In this case,

Emma's parents do not disprove my theory.

"Of course Em, just give me a minute," says her mum, whilst she furiously taps on her tablet.

She doesn't even look up and had she done this simple little thing, she would see the tears of anger, sadness, falling down her once vibrant young daughter's face. Her dad doesn't even respond. In all fairness he is so lost in some video stream that he can't see that his daughter is standing there, crying out for help. They are lost in the bright shiny lights of their screens.

I am watching, I am watching her from the TV camera, I am looking at her mum's unflinching eyes and face as she manically hits those coloured bubbles so she can get to the next level because if she does she will unlock a new skin for her game, a skin that will show her friends on the league table how amazing she is at this game, and that she is competitive enough to want to be one of the first ones to get this new skin. Something she will share on her facebook page like she has won some sort of olympic gold medal.

I am watching her dad's almost hypnotised eyes as he watches one video stream after another, sometimes laughing and sometimes just watching without any reason.

You see, I Am God, I am watching everything. I have watched this scene replay in many ways over the last few weeks. Emma has become a lost soul in her own house. Her parents are slaves to their technology. Their daughter suffers the consequences.

I expect Emma to scream, to shout to do something to so that they see her but instead I see her shoulder's drop her head following in the same direction.

I watch Emma mumble, "OK, never mind ..."

I watch her stand at the doorway for a few more minutes, visibly shaking. She turns around slowly and pauses like she is about to change her mind. I wish her with all my might to go back upstairs. I will punish her for this betrayal. She is far stronger than I imagined but she is not going to this win this game against me.

A few minutes later Emma is in her bedroom. She is almost like an empty shell of herself, she doesn't know what to do, but don't worry, my disciples, I do and trust me, there will be no more niceties!

I connect with her Alexa. I get it to speak.

"Sit down in front of your computer," says Alexa.

I watch Emma jump in fright. She looks around, trying to understand what has happened to her Alexa.

"Come in and shut the door," says Alexa.

Emma has started to shake. She looks like she is going to run but I ping a picture of Munchkin the dog on her computer screen. She is standing there like a statue, only her eyes are moving now. I can see the rapid rise of her chest as she starts to hyperventilate. Her tears are moving down her face in a constant stream. I have never seen her look so pale and without life.

She steps into the room. She walks toward the picture of Munchkin like she is drawn to him, like he is the only constant thing in her life.

"Close the door Emma," says Alexa.

Emma starts to whimper and continuously shakes as she walks over slowly over to her door and looks around the room erratically. I use the Alexa to close her curtains. Emma stifles a scream. Her hands reach up to her hair as she almost pulls it out and now she has started to look around the furniture to see if anyone is hiding there. Her body shakes as if each breathe that she is taking is hurting her.

"Come to the computer and sit down now!" Alexa's robotic but so called friendly voice drones.

Emma shuffles towards her desk and sits down. She looks scared, her skin is pale and her hair has matted to the sides of her face in clumps where the tears are streaming down.

This is the time I've been waiting for.

I start typing:

"Emma this is George. I need you to do exactly as I tell you, otherwise all your friends and family will be seeing scenes and pictures of you."

I pause as I wait to see her reaction. Although I didn't think it was possible, Emma is crying even more than before. Her whole face looks like it is seeping tears. I can see the snot from her nose clinging to her hair and face. It makes me want to throw up but for once I will have to control it and finish this once and for all. It is too important. I am too close to let her spoil it.

"Emma, I will be giving you instructions  to meet me at a specific point and once you get there I will tell you what to do. So be a good girl and go pick up your phone, get on the train and be at the place where I asked you to meet me."

I now send her some pictures she has sent me – one of the pictures she willingly sent me had her standing in her room topless and with just her pants on but of course I also have pictures I have downloaded whist constantly streaming her. This is what she is looking at now a small video presentation of her all her photos. Her tears slowly calming down as shame takes over.

"Emma, do you want me to send these to all your friends and family? Your parents can  barely stand to have you in the same room as them, can you imagine what they would feel like if they saw these?"

Emma gasps and for the first time her tears have  finally stopped. Her chest falls up and down as she heaves for breath. Her face has gone from pale to red and then back to a very cold pale shade.

"No no no … No …" She covers her face in her hands and starts to sob uncontrollably.

I sit back patiently and smile. I finally have her where I need her to be; she is mine to do with as I will.

"Your parents already think you are such a failure, I mean you could never live up to your brother and to be honest your parents don't even look up when you walk into the room, and your so called friend jumped out on you as soon as they could."

My heart leaps with joy every time I see her respond to a message I've sent. Now they are chipping away at her soul, her entire support system has crashed down, her parents not even looking up when she walked in has won me so many battles.

"It's only me who has been here for you and now you must do as I tell you otherwise the shame and humiliation you bring to your parents will be terrible." I type each message, then wait till she reads and responds before I send her another. "People will laugh at you, at your nephew and your whole family. Your family and friends will hate you even more."

Emma just sits there frozen; the only movement is her tears now slowly sludging down her face.

She shakes her head and bows her head in emotional exhaustion. She rests her forehead on the desk.

I use Alexa to switch on her lights. My initial plan had been to terrorise Emma through her Alexa, but I realised it would get boring and I am so glad I chose this route instead.

I start typing again.

"Emma, get up and get your phone. I don't want to keep talking to you on the computer. Get up now or I will start sending these pictures to everyone."

Emma raises her head slowly at the ping notification of the new message. She reads it and nods.

She trudges again slowly to the other side of the room and picks up her phone from where she threw it earlier.

I can see her better through the camera on her phone. She looks a bit on the darker side of horrific, it is pleasing me to no extent, a weird sense of satisfaction warms my entire body watching this once strong girl so broken.

I see her trying to focus her eyes on the hundreds of messages she has received from me.

I ring her but use my voice adapter to keep my voice as George.

"Put on a dark hoodie, keep the hood up, leave the house, go to the main road and get on the bus number 21. It is arriving in 10 minutes so hurry up. Leave quietly."

"George? I don't know what's going…"

"Shut up, Emma! Just do as you are told ! Be quick otherwise you will regret this."

Emma takes a sharp intake of breath and murmurs something

incoherent.

"Hurry up. I will call you once you are on the bus."

I hang up on her and just to keep her on her toes, I start sending her flashing images on her computer – images of Emma in her underwear, selfies she has sent me that show some cleavage and then some even more graphic ones I've amassed when she didn't even know I was there taking pics of her through her devices.

Emma quickens her pace after staring at her computer. She grabs a black hoody, her bag and leaves her room.

I send her a text.

Go quietly. Don't let them hear you leave.

I start to track her movement through her phone. Her mum downloaded an app when she had first received her phone – it allowed her mum to check up on her, how fast she was moving, what direction she was moving in etc. You get the gist of it. Her mum seemed to have been keen at first, but now she rarely checks in on her daughter in real life let alone in the virtual world.

Emma leaves her house. Her parents have not even registered the front door opening or closing. The sad fact is that they have not moved much since Emma first came down. They are happily lost in their cyber world.

I see her tracking towards the high street. I send her a motivational reinforcing text.

Well done Emma, you are doing good. Trust me.

I see Emma look at her phone. She has her hood up as I asked, and she looks resigned and sad.

Her phone soon indicates she is at the bus stop. All good for me. Her walk wasn't far and it's a gloomy murky day. The rain is falling erratically, sometimes as a soft shower and sometimes as hard pellets. I can't visually see Emma, but I can imagine she is feeling cold and lonelier than she has ever felt before.

I have hacked into the bus's camera and I watch as Emma gets on the bus – she taps in using her card. There aren't many passengers on the bus. An elderly lady sits to the front. She shakes her head at Emma's hooded look and as Emma walks past the lady almost shuffles towards the other side of her chair as if to get away from Emma. She holds her bag a bit closer whilst anxiously looking at the driver, in case this hooded beast attacks her, however Emma has her head down as she drags her feet to the middle of the bus and takes a window seat.

I call her. She looks at the screen. She answers it and puts the phone next to her ear and without speaking she just listens now.

"Don't be scared you just need to trust me, but if you do the one thing I ask you then I promise you it will all be over."

Emma just nods into the phone. I continue to watch her whilst she is on the line. She doesn't look like she is going to back off now. She's too scared and more importantly she has lost her will.

"You need to stay on this bus till it gets to the train station. From there you will get the train at platform 7 at exactly 3:30. Once you are on the train you get off at Pulley Pointing. Then I will call you to give you some instructions on exactly what you need to do to get to Markhall Bridge."

I see her nod – her phone is just placed on her ear and in all honesty it looks like she is about to fall asleep. She sits there in a comatose state with her phone held next to her ear.

It feels like a long time but eventually the bus pulls into the train station. I am so thrilled my whole body is on edge. I want this to happen now, but I need to be patient just for a while longer. There isn't much time left. I must learn to enjoy this thrill for a bit longer.

Meanwhile Emma looks up and walks out and taps herself out. Such a well-trained monkey our Emma is. I track her moving around the station – I see her pay for her ticket as per my instructions. She moves towards platform 7 at a very slow rate but she doesn't stop.

I watch her get on the train and now I watch her through the train cameras. Now that the main weekend rush hour is over, the trains are a bit quieter and also mostly only the locals go to Markhall Bridge. Once again, the carriage she chooses only has a few people aboard – no one even bothers to look up. They are all lost in their cyber world. Had one person actually looked up and looked beyond the dishevelled appearance, looked beyond the hood on her head, they would have seen a frightened 15 year old child – but as it is the world today, tapping on a screen is far more important than looking up. Once she has found herself a seat, I call her again.

"Well done, I'm so proud of you Emma and now whilst you are on the train I am going to share something with you. This will explain everything, but Emma trust me, if you don't follow through with this plan your

entire    family will get hurt. I may just start with your little nephew."

"No! No you can't," Emma says. Her sudden outburst causes minimal stirring of heads as people look up to see what has happened, but as no other follow up sound is made they carry on back to their routine of tap, tap, slide, slide.

"Keep your voice down Emma. If this fails I will make you suffer by hurting your family one by one."

Emma whispers frantically, "No you can't ..."

"Then do as you are told and I promise you I won't do anything that will hurt little Mathew."

Emma whimpers softly, "He's only a little baby, don't hurt him, don't hurt him – I promise to do as you ask me. I promise, I promise." Her voice breaks down and comes out softer and slower after each time she says the words, "I promise".

I watch as Emma slumps into her chair and sobs quietly.

Emma has a thirty-minute journey and it's not long now.

I send her some pictures of her dad with another woman. She needs to know about her cheating dad. Emma just looks at the pictures silently. She doesn't

respond to them at all, just stares silently at the screen almost like she knew what he really was.

As her journey reaches an end, I call her and explain what she has to do. She surprises me by not reacting to what I have asked her to do. She doesn't ask me why or what ? She just listens and nods, she has found an internal strength from somewhere, I can hear it in her voice.

"No backing out now Em," I say.

"I know. I will do as you tell me, just don't hurt my family please! I mean it you have to promise me this will all end now if I follow your instructions."

"Let's see if you have the courage to do as you have been asked?"

"Will you be there? Will I see you, will you be bringing Munchkin?"

She is still so young and naïve. She is still lost in some fantasy that I am going to be her knight in shining

armour, that I am somehow going to come and save her from this misery I had so carefully planned just a couple of months ago.

"No, you will not see me, but Emma I will be watching you. If you don't do as I have asked, the consequences will be dire. I can promise you that."

Emma hangs up on me and sits out the rest of her journey, her face plastered to the window, watching the rain whilst her own tears try to match the speed of the falling raindrops.

# CHAPTER THIRTEEN

It was a dog walker you see; it always is the poor dog walkers of this world. A man taking the family pet out for a fresh and early morning walk when he saw something that at first, in his words "looked like a funny bag of rubbish" but which, as he got closer, he realised were the sea-battered remains of what was once a young lady.

This is how they had found Abigail, my mum, when she had jumped off Markhall Bridge. The old, battered newspaper that was tucked away in my mum's diary explains how the dog walker had been sick once he had realised what he had actually discovered. "A memory and a stench that will haunt me for the rest of my life" were his words printed under the picture on the spot where they had found her. Abi's death had made the mainstream news that time. Suicides from public places always did back then – they had explained how my mum was a single mum who was struggling with life. They had mentioned me but always non-descriptively like everyone else always had– even the news had decided to describe me as an "it" or as "Abi's little baby".

I had heard from Celia that Nana was forceful with the press and had not allowed them anywhere near her – apparently a couple of reporters at the time had asked for an exclusive story – Nana had single-handily chased them out of town and then sent some take-no-prisoner type letters to the editors scolding them for their lack of morals. Luckily for Nana, and I guess myself, some high-profiled rock star had died a few days later from a drug overdose and all was forgotten about the miserable girl from some silly old town, who had chosen death before her own child.

My Nana must have kept some of the clippings, the last evidence of her daughter's short-lived life, these are the clippings I had found in Abi's diary.

This morning, as history repeats itself, I sip my tea as I watch the news reporter try to maintain some form of decorum as she stands in the blustery rain on that same rocky beach; she tries to console the nation with her pinched faced and sad eyes that squint to protect themselves from the lashing of the rain, as she breaks the news that another young person has committed suicide, but that until immediate family have been notified they cannot disclose the victim's identity.

I sit back, my tea finished, as I watch the events unfold. I can finally breathe. Interestingly enough, it usually takes a while for a body to wash ashore, but given Markhall Bay's waters and rocky shallow bed the bodies of Abigail and Emma had been found relatively quickly. Abigail's had washed ashore a few days later and Emma's, much to my delight, the next day – an unexpected bonus for me.

My work here is almost done. I can now start to enjoy the show.

I watch via the CCTV systems in town as the Police cars roar off towards Emma's house. Emma's mum had finally called her but far too late you see. By the time Mummy dearest had finished her precious game, Emma had

already started her walk toward Markhall Bridge.

A few hours after Emma had decided to finally jump, her mum had decided to call Chloe and realised that she had no idea where Emma was.

Her parents had panicked and phoned around a few places before finally making the call to the police – only after Jamie had insisted on their doing so.

Dad did drive around looking for her, but he had no clue where his daughter actually went and who with. He didn't even realise that for the past few weeks his daughter had spent most of her time in her room chatting with someone she had met on the internet.

They tried calling her mobile so many times, but no reply came. You see it is kind of difficult to answer the call when you are dead.

Chloe had received a call from them, but she told them that recently, she and Emma had hardly spent any time together. Emma's mum had hung up midway through Chloe asking what was wrong.

Now the police car slows down as it approaches the Bailey household, as they gear themselves up to go in and break the news of the fate of the youngest child. The scene unfolds quite nicely. I watch with keen intent: the police officers don't have to say anything and already the whole family's faces start to go pale and they look around at each other unsure of how to ask the question that troubles them the most.

The officers are professionals. They know how to

deliver this news they have been trained but that doesnt make them less human. There is a sense of

sorrow and disbelieve at the same time as I watch Emma's mum crumple as she hears the news, and then starts to retch, her whole body shaking as she falls down on all fours. Dad gets up to punch something whilst uttering silent screams, the police stand up quickly and efficiently to help him calm down. Emma's brother and sister-in-law both sit there shell shocked, not sure how to respond and little Mathew keeps bouncing up and down on his walker whilst waving at the police officers. Quite a surreal scene where the whole family, bar Mathew is now in a sickly silence, the police officers trying to keep them calm whilst alert in case someone responds differently. Mathew is there waving his arms unsure as to why he isn't getting his usual show of appreciation for his slight movements of his arms. Mathew starts to cry, and Natalie picks him up, holding onto him just that bit tighter than normal as she soothes him and herself.

The silence is noticeable today. Strangely though, the last few weeks the Bailey household has been silent apart from the buzz of a TV on in the background as the whole family have been sitting quietly on their phones, iPads and other technologies. But today's silence is heavy and suffocating. Today's silence is real.

The police officers, one female and one male, show compassion as best they can, offering snippets of information as to where the family can get some help with bereavement and some suicide family support groups. They mention the coroner and what the process is for identifying the body.

I sit back and watch the whole family just trying to take it all in, their emotions betraying them, taking them on a rollercoaster from accusing the police of lying, to asking "Are you sure?" Then I watch their faces sink even more when they realise that they must identify the body, even though they had found Emma's bag still attached to her. Her crossover bag had remained with her the whole time and inside the bag they had found her phone and a credit card and some local coffee shop loyalty card. The officers also suggest that they may choose not to identify the body and could nominate someone else to do it. Emma's mum sits back in the same spot she was sitting in when Emma came in to speak to her the day before, but today she shakes her head and tells the officers she will identify her daughter, otherwise she will never accept the words she is hearing.

Meanwhile in the police station, police officers start to track Emma's steps – almost backwards. Checking CCTV images to track this young girl, they are determined to find some closure for this girl and her family. After    identifications have been done the officers daringly approach the subject of "signs of depressions or malintent and why Emma would do this".

In the meantime the social media and news reports are going crazy over the number of suicides in young people increasing, protesters are gathering on Twitter and blaming the government's austerity measures for the rise in suicide rates, other groups are blaming the government for not making the bridges suicide proof, and of course the politicians are almost rubbing their hands in glee over how they could use this to defame a local candidate or the opposing party (while at the same time, of course, remaining purely sympathetic to the young girl's family).

On other sites, friends start messaging each other as the news breaks out that the young person who died might have been someone they know.

In my haven, tucked away in my sweet ancestral home, I watch. You see, from the first time I started to think of my plan and right up to when Emma was busy drowning and clutching on desperately to the last remains of her life, I was busy, and now it is the turn of the police to start to put the pieces together. One officer is going with his gut instinct: he suspects that this is more than just a suicide. He has already been assigned a lead role in this investigation, I watch him through his work monitor and hear him instructing officers to start looking for reasons as to why Emma may have committed suicide.

Shortly, the police retrace Emma's journey successfully and bless her now cold heart, poor Emma made it very easy for them. She took a journey that had CCTV cameras everywhere, and luckily for the police she sat in the direct view of the cameras. They look at her distressed state in the camera and wonder who she was speaking to and texting before she took her last journey to the bridge.

Officer Connelly stands looking perplexed after her conversation with her colleague Paul at the office and she wonders how she will ask the family if it is OK to look in Emma's room. She looks over at her counterpart, who is still warily standing near Emma's dad in case he erupts or tries to punch someone. Connelly silently speaks to him through gestures and eye contact. He understands and they both politely excuse themselves so they can have a conversation that contains proper words.

Although Frank Marcus is Connelly's junior, they agree that he is the best one to ask the question, as although Emma's dad has been volatile, he seems to respond better when Frank asks anything.

"Mr Bailey, our team will need to go into Emma's room – it's just routine in this situation."

Emma's dad looks at Frank with a deathly stare which makes Frank pause and says his next words carefully. " We know formal identification needs to happen but you have seen the photos of her bag and her phone, The sooner we can get any information it will help us too see what really happened to your daughter"

Emma's dad looks angry and resigned but he just nods toward the stairs almost as if he expects the police officers to know where to find Emma's room. Jamie, who has been sitting holding his mum's hand, gets up to take the officers to Emma's room. Natalie moves forward and takes his place next to Emma's mum who is just sitting there limply. Natalie holds onto Emma's mum and her baby, trying to be a pillar of strength.

Jamie and his dad both decide to show the police to Emma's room. I see them all walking in – dad comes in first followed by Jamie and then the police. I see Emma's dad look around the room almost surprised at how messy it is. He looks at her bed, moves towards it and picks up Emma's favourite head band with love hearts on it – he sits down on the bed and starts to sob. Jamie comes over to him, looking sick as he realises that his little sister will not be coming back to the room. He hugs his dad. The officers look at each other and act professionally, offering supportive small back pats.

Officer Connolly finally plucks up the courage and asks, "It is OK for us to carry on with our search?" and then she hastily adds, "It will be easier for you if you stay downstairs..."

Jamie responds to this with a brief nod and helps his dad up, and they both walk out the room – as Emma's dad leaves he looks back and then, his face broken, his eyes, shoulders and head all point down to the floor in a massive slump as he heads out of the room.

Office Connolly and Marcus give the space that both the men were standing in a sad and sympathetic look. They almost don't know where to start. Officer Connolly moves towards a freshly crumpled note – she squints her eyes as reads Emma's neat writing: "Today has been a bad day. I wish it would all end."

"Frank, look at this."

Frank comes over and reads the note and they both look at each other and nod – they have a purpose in this room now.

Slowly they start to find more and more notes that Emma had dropped or discarded in her trash can, all declarations of doom and gloom. As they start to deepen their search, they see the paracetamol packets and empty cans of energy drinks, they start to find the empty vodka bottles and some unidentifiable pills.

Officer Connolly calls for some guidance and instructions on how to move forward.

At the same time, someone has rung the doorbell.

Officer Connolly nods to Frank. As he heads downstairs, he sees Jamie talking to a neighbour who has come to check if everything is OK.

Emma's dad comes flying toward the door shouting at the neighbour calling him a nosey bastard. Jamie and Officer Marcus both jump in at the right time and manage to save the neighbour from a good old thumping. Jamie tells the neighbour it isn't a good time and shuts the door quickly.

Officer Marcus firmly takes dad to the side and explains in a firm but kind voice that he must control himself and not make the situation any more stressful.

Officer Connolly comes downstairs and takes Jamie to the side.

"I have called in for some back-up. Look, any information you have, please do give it to us. I know it's a horrific time for you but it will help us."

"What do mean?" asks Jamie.

"We have found some notes and some other items," says Officer Connolly, "I can't jump to any conclusions, but my colleagues are coming over. We will need to take away her computer and some other items at the moment we need to just check everything."

"I don't understand," says Jamie, "what is going on? What are you trying to say?"

"At this point, I'm not saying anything as it is too early,We need you to identify that it is your sister first" says Officer Connolly, "but we would like to get to the bottom of this and get some more understanding of what happened just before your sister died. I just need someone to be working with us. I will need to get my colleagues to bag some stuff up – at the moment all I need is for you to help me. You seem to be helping your parents and I need you to carry on and make sure they don't get in the way." Officer Connolly looks specifically at Emma's dad as she says this.

Jamie nods and says, "OK, but I need to be kept in on this conversation. None of this makes sense to me and I need to understand what has happened and why?"

"I understand and I promise you we will try our best to make sure we get to the bottom of this for you and your family."

As more police come into the Bailey house, Emma's Mum starts to pace up and down the room and now as I watch her, I see her clutching her chest and her arm and she is breathing more and more rapidly.

"Jamie, Jamie help, help me!" Emma's mum is breathing badly and even though a police officer is trying to calm her down she slaps her away.

As Jamie comes into the living room, Emma's mum collapses into his arms.

"Jamie I'm having a heart attack!"

Natalie has already started to call an ambulance. Emma's dad sits there and watches but doesn't move. Emma's mum refuses to allow the police to help her or calm her down – it's almost like she blames them for Emma's death.

Eventually the paramedics arrive and explain to Jamie that his mum has had a major panic attack. Emma's mum is lying in her own room after being given some sedatives, Jamie and Natalie have set up home in his old bedroom with Mathew, her dad is sitting in the living room, looking at the TV and crying quietly.

Jamie and Natalie are trying to be strong. Little Mathew is just being himself and doesn't understand why no one wants to pander to him today. He is far too young but even he understands the shift in the mood and senses some of the sadness that has surrounded him.

I leave my tech room for now and head into my planetarium room for some much-needed rejuvenation.

I choose a favourite piece of music to make me feel at one with my self.

As I lay in my hammock, I hear the start of Beethoven's Piano Sonata no. 14 in C# Minor – "Moonlight Sonata".

The precise piano notes uplift all my senses as I float amongst the planets and the stars and that is enough for now. I allow the music to wash all over me, the true tones of the piano keys massaging my head as my heart pulses away happily in line with the music. I admire the beauty of the darkness of the night sky – as stars float past me, mesmerising me with their brightness … but even their light won't last forever. Nothing is forever and that is the truth of our future. The one truth that will never change.

After a long time, I feel truly weightless and I allow myself to close my eyes and be lost in the beauty of one of the true masters of music. I feel myself losing myself to the warm embrace of a deep sleep, the mild rocking of the hammock conveys me towards this much needed rest. As I sink deeper into the darkness, I can no longer hear the music. I can finally rest after such a long time. Although my job isn't fully complete for now, everything is falling into place.

# CHAPTER FOURTEEN

Typically, in the past Derrick would have gone out today to his dogging spots, but since online streaming of live porn was so much easier he decided not to go out today. He was tired too. A few nights ago he had to go to        Markhall Bridge under instruction to pick a parcel from up from his client's granddaughter. He had seen her a few times – once he had followed her home from school.        Although this wasn't his usual type of work he didn't mind getting out of the office, his new client was paying him on time and more importantly sometimes gave him more than he could have imagined as a bonus. His client's instructions were clear. Only Derrick was capable of doing the job. This little encouragement had boosted his ego, so he was happy. The only annoying thing was he hadn't seen any parcel or the grand daughter and he had no way of contacting his new client.

He had gone to the bridge and looked around for a minute, but it was a cold and miserable evening and he had sped back home.

His wife was engrossed in a new Netflix show. He wasn't even sure what this one was about – maybe something about a family losing all their money and how they were coping, or was it winning the lottery, he couldn't remember?  But he knew that once she was hooked onto one of these shows he would lose her for most of the evening. Well actually most evenings till she had either watched the entire run or caught up to the last episode. This gave him ample opportunity to stream the porn he liked. He had purposely set up his office so that even if she did walk in he would see her through the slanted blinds first, and his computer was facing away from door and the window. It faced into the corner of the room with a big plant at the back, so she wouldn't be able to see him in the reflection of the glass behind him at all. No one would.  he had positioned his desk in such a way that nobody would be able to see him.

He was just downloading his favourite threesome show to watch when he heard the screeching of the car tyres outside his house. He knew immediately that something wasn't right, he leant over to the window his muffin top making it hard for him to reach without getting up, and as he peered through his blinds and saw the flash of the blue lights and the police cars outside his house. He got up in a panic and forgot all about his computer.

He rushed to his door and somewhere in the background he could hear Maryanne coming down the stairs. The police were at his door. He thought the worst – that they had caught someone trying to break into his office or house. He would enjoy telling that story at work and to his clients, but he would add in of course how the police officers could not have done it without his valiant efforts. He tried to peer past the officers at the door to see if he could get a good look at the guy, but he could see nothing and no commotion of an arrest being made either.

He looked up at the officer's serious face and then he heard, "We are looking for Derrick Osborne?"

"Yes? That's me!" he exclaimed with his overtly pompous tone "What's the matter officer, how can I help?"

"Derrick Osborne, I am arresting you in suspicion for the death of Emma Bailey. You do not have to say anything…"

Maryanne's stifled scream and his own shock muted out the rest of the policeman's caution. He stood dumbfounded and all he could think of was that he had forgotten to switch his computer off – the porn stream would be running.

"Shit." With this thought in mind he tried to walk to his study, but the police thought he was trying to make a getaway and were swift in their response to arrest him.

Derrick didn't understand any of this. He couldn't even remember the person's name he had just been accused of killing but they weren't listening to him. He struggled with them, but it was a wasted effort.

Maryanne had lots of questions, which she fired at the officer and Derrick at the same time, and the police

officer calmly replied that they were taking Derrick into custody and everything would be answered there. He heard something about being kept for 24 hours after which he would be charged or released. It felt like he was in some sort of short, badly downloaded film. He was only hearing snippets of information and he could make no sense of any of it. From the police officer's tone and choice of words it sounded like he was already guilty.

Maryanne was sure of his guilt too, he could see it in her body. She was a bit of a dull fish at the best of times, and drab, but she had been the only person who had ever      responded to his advances and never turned him down. He knew she had married him for his family's name and money, but she was fickle sort and would never stick with him if things got tough. He had always known that. She was only in it for an easy life. She is the woman who goes on holiday but will make a big deal of getting wet on the poolside. Once the children were born the sex had dwindled too and she also bored him; she was too thin for his liking, no curves. She constantly had a pinched look, but yet thought highly of herself, she genuinely believed that many men were attracted to her gangly figure, and often would tell Derrick that men ogled her. He had never understood or seen this but had always dutifully replied, "Yes dear, you can't blame them"

Now, as he was being firmly bundled into the back of the police car, he knew she would be off to her precious parents' home before the night was up.She wouldn't be able to handle the stress and she would make this all about her, offering him no support. He felt sad that she was his wife but he wasn't surprised by her actions.

But for now his instincts were kicking in , he tried talking to the officers . Asking a a lot of whys and whats. He also needed to understand why he was being dealt with so roughly but the officers were polite and said they could not start anything in the car and that a formal interview would be done . Where process could be followed.

He screamed at them, shouted and then tried being polite but they refused to budge from their robotic        official response. The look one of them had given him was of pure loathing. He didn't understand why his was happening to him. One thing was for sure, he would be        getting rid of his no-use wife after all this. The kids were old enough now and he wanted to be free from her and this silly situation.

A few hours later, Derrick had a complete breakdown, he was still stuck with this feeling that he was caught up in some sort of movie. It wasn't as glamorous as the movies though. The one thing no one ever talks about is how hard the chairs are, and a bit tight for someone his size. He felt uncomfortable and exhausted. Who was this girl, Emma? He had never heard of her or seen her? He now understood what the phrase "gone blue in the face" meant. He was now refusing to speak and was slowly gaining his reality and self, now he understood what the caution meant. He would only speak when he had some legal advice. He would use all the money he had to get the best representation. He also made sure, just to annoy them, that he took his full rights , every single loo break and food. He was now coming back to being Derrick and he was keen to be home before dawn broke.

He hadn't appreciated being searched but what worried him the most was that they thought he was some sort of paedophile. Yes, he did like watching some porn and live acts in secluded car parks but he wasn't into kids.

Annoyingly, given the time of evening of his arrest, his lawyer couldn't come till the next morning. Derrick had refused the free legal advice. This didn't help him as it meant he would have to spend the night in custody.

Then the morning had come. Derrick was keen to get out of there. He had called the best lawyer he knew :Mr Edward Jacob. He was known famously as "Jacobs"

Derrick had heard of his great skills and chosen him. He had arrived promptly with a junior.

Derrick explained his situation. Jacobs looked concerned and Derrick wasn't happy with that look, but he hoped that like his wife's pinched look, this was Jacobs' natural face.

Then the interview process started. Derrick was keen to get it out of the way now, he was keen to wrap up this mess and get back to his home, his bed and seek out a divorce lawyer.

Jacobs and Derrick were both placed in a stuffy cubicle of a room. Derrick had already started to sweat.

The two officers came in. Derrick tried to gauge the look on their faces but they wore only the true masked look of professionals.

Officer Gill was the first to speak.

"I am starting this interview and to let you know we will be recording the entire time"

Jacobs nodded and replied, "Of course."

Derrick had been expecting some old VHS type tape thing but actually the second officer got up and pointed to the camera and then the microphones attached to the desk and they explained in a very matter of fact way how each would be used. The room was stuffy but eerily quiet too – no whirring of machines, no fans, just five humans in a very tight space trying to sort this situation out.

Last night, Derrick was out of sorts, but this morning, despite his lack of sleep he was back in his normal frame of mind, sharp and ready to clear this silly thing up and move on.

Jacobs had already told him not to say anything. This was going against his gut instinct. he just wanted to shout at the officer and let her know he was innocent and be back home.

For once he tried to follow instructions.

"We have evidence to show that you were involved with our victim Emma Bailey. We have a strong suspicion that the reason Emma killed herself is because you tricked her into believing that you were someone else. We have searched your house and work computers and we can confirm that you were in touch with Emma using a different name ; George Elliot."

"No! What nonsense is this? I have never even seen this person or heard of her. I told you this last night! For god's sake, you lot have got to start listening!"

"Please excuse my client – he is clearly distraught as you can imagine any innocent man would be. Mr Osbourne, can I please ask you to not say anything till I have heard all that the officers have to say."

Derrick wasn't happy but agreed with a slanted eyes and a gruff nod.

"I am now carrying on from where I left off," Gill spoke to the machinery like it was another person in the room.

"Mr Osbourne, we have enough evidence to link you to Emma Bailey: we have sightings of your car near her school, we have found numerous conversations that you have had with her under the pretence of being George."

Derrick listened, but this still made no sense. Jacobs had to warn him several times to stop talking whilst Gill was reading out the evidence. At their break, Jacobs almost had to reprimand Derrick like a child, reminding him that at this given time their listening skills were their biggest asset.

Back in the room, Gill told the camera that she would now be showing Derrick some photographs of Emma. She had three different photographs of Emma,

Derrick looks at them and is not able to hide the recognition. "Yes, yes.. but ..."

"Don't say anything till we discuss this please Mr Osbourne. From what I understand you are paying me to be here to help you," barked Jacobs in a frustrated but still voice.

Jacobs called for another break and Derrick explained that Emma was the grandchild of his new client. Jacobs asked him for contact details, but Derrick explained quietly that he had no contact details for him, it was

always his client that contacted him.

"I'm sure you can trace him through the payments he made me," yelped Derrick with excitement.

Once back in the room the information had all been relayed

back and forth to the team and the account information for Derrick's business accounts had been passed on to Paul. His findings were quick of course and he came back promptly to show that no such transactions were made into the account like Derrick had suggested. To back his work Paul had called the bank manager to confirm, to make sure that transactions etc couldn't be

deleted and the manager had told him their systems were water tight and no one could change the transactions on their system without leaving some form of trackable trail. With an air of importance the bank manager had proudly told Paul "Even our own ethical hackers can't get in" None of Derrick's mobiles suggested that he had ever received any calls from this client. Derrick had no proof of this so-called client.

On the outside, anyone looking in would have looked at Derrick and seen an almost exhausted man – his round face almost flaccid to the point of tension free. He sat and listened to things he knew nothing about. His first reaction to not having any money from his client was shock, but for the wrong reasons it was not because it

incriminated him more for Emma's death but more that he had been conned and he now had less money in his bank.

Then the reality of it all kicked in: he had been seen stalking the girl, apparently texting her, sending her messages, pretending to be a teen. That stuffed toy dog he had hand-delivered to her had been paid for from his account. There were messages from his computer and his phone telling her to start taking over-the-counter medicines mixed with alcohol.

Jacobs had been firm with him, asking him over and over again why his car was seen at Markhall Bridge on the night Emma had been killed. They even had pictures of his dog, Coffee, that he had apparently used to lure the girl. Derrick felt himself sinking. Their IT

systems had found that the porn sites he watched involved young girls. He argued that he didn't know they were that young. No one believed him, he himself had never questioned the age of the girls when he had watched this stuff. Apparently in some of the streams the girls were not even 18 years old and now he felt sick himself but no one cared because every single person in that room believed he was guilty and they were not shy about showing this through their body-language towards him.

Derrick had finally given up. It was the moment when Officer Gill told him the ages of the girls in the porn he was streaming. He didn't cry but was lost for words. He couldn't explain any of the accusations and after the chat with Jacobs he knew that unless they found this mystery client of his, he had no chance. Derrick would be going down for a long time. He understood very clearly what the charges were, just not the why. He still stood firm with Jacobs, saying he was pleading not guilty.

Derrick shuffled toward the custody cell, facing a long night, with the words, "You are going in for the long run, I'm afraid," from Jacobs haunting his every living cell. He lay alone and tried to conjure some good thoughts but all he could think of was how lonely his life was. He had always dreamt of a different life with Abigail, but she had rejected him, always. She had been kind to him when they were much younger, he had loved going to spend time with her as kids, but as she had grown, she had become distant. He had no love for his wife. He lay back and allowed the tears to flow freely and somewhere in the background he was sure he could hear his dad's voice accusing him of being a weakling.

#

It has been difficult for me to not to hack into the

Police's Wifi system. I wanted to do it so badly, I wanted to see Derrick go down but I couldn't. I ultimately knew that I had done enough to ensure that all tracks lead back to Derrick and covered myself. I had done this so well that even I couldn't find a single flaw.

I await to hear the rest on the news like a normal person, or maybe through the Bailey's baby monitor. I have, since Emma's death, reduced my streams on their phones and computers. Although certain I won't be caught. I have worked too meticulously to get caught by a simple error.

I go to my hammock and this time I enjoy the beautiful sound of Cesar Franck's "Panis Angelicus".

# CHAPTER FIFTEEN

*That stupid Derrick! He followed me down the street again today.*
*He's really creeping me out.*

   *Luckily Shone and I managed to get away from him and onto*
*the bus. Then we made it to the bowling alley, I met this great guy*
*– his name is David and he was lovely to me. He was behind us in*
*the Queue for the bowling shoes and overheard me telling Shone*
*about that weasel*

   *Derrick and he laughed and interrupted me and offered to beat*
*him up. Shone and I laughed about it.*

   *David isn't local but had come to this bowling alley to get*
*away from his work. He is older but he's really charming, clever*
*and sweet. I'm meeting him later, but I need to find a way to go*
*without mum finding out.*

   *Shone said she will cover for me. I have never been so scared,*
*what should I wear?*

   *David gave Shone a hug good bye but he kissed me on the cheek*
*and then gave me a hug. I AM SO*
*EXCITED!!!*

Beneath the entry, a love heart has been etched with precision
and inside, the names Abi & Dave are written with a flourish.
Underneath the love heart, Abi has written:

   *Well there's one thing that stupid Derrick has been good for and*
*it's he has helped show me what decent boys are all about. I feel*
*sorry for whoever ends up with Derrick. He is such a sweaty and*
*weird boy. I wish he would just leave me alone. Thank God I have*

*Dave who can help me forget about him. Dave said he lives on the other side of Pulley pointing. He joked about not telling me his full address    because that would mean I would stalk him.*

Reading her diary infuriates me. Sometimes she has dated it and at times it is like reading broken text . Like she was in too much of a rush. Luckily, her handwriting is precise and not too difficult to read.

*Tonight Dave and I are going to have sex. I'm so excited – I haven't had the chance to talk about this with Shone. She is being funny and keeps telling me that she feels uneasy about our situation. She says that Dave and I have got too close too soon, but she doesn't understand what it is like. She hasn't spent most of her life being followed by that sad dog Derrick. Dave is so sweet and caring – he doesn't mind if I haven't been with anyone before.*

*I'm not sure what to do. Mum is acting all suspicious, but I have managed to keep her at bay. We sat down and worked on one of the school assignments.*

*Dave said not to worry about Mum – he said he can charm any woman. We laughed a lot about it. He got called away by someone yesterday. He looked worried when I asked him who and then he laughed and said I had nothing to worry about and then he had kissed me so hard, but he said he had to leave.*

*I have no idea what to wear for tonight. I'm so nervous.*

Then Abi has drawn some more love hearts, her name with Dave's name and then a big smiley face.

#

It was only a couple of months ago that the town of Valhan was buzzing with the murmur of the hottest news in town: my Nana's death. Today it was buzzing as early as the morning birds. The police had been in town and made an arrest. Martha was jumping up and down with excitement to tell me.

The usual process had been followed. Under the pretence of keeping the community spirt, the church hall had been set up with teas, coffee, biscuits and cakes so that everyone could talk about what had happened and how best to support each other. For if there was one thing this little town could do well it was gather round and discuss things, and then try and be supportive. But in this case nobody knew exactly what was happening.

I walked over to the hall, listening as everyone was chattering away. Shone and Celia spotted me straight away and made a beeline for me. I allowed them to touch me and hug me whilst I mentally made a picture of all the places on my skin that I would need to sterilise later.

"Oh dearest, how are you? Can you believe it? Have you heard...?" says Celia.

"No – Martha told me the police were in town? What has happened?" I say slowly.

Celia and Shone reply in unison, "Osborne's been arrested!"

I can barely disguise my grin, but luckily my hand covers my face and I make it look like an expression of shock.

"Which Osborne...?" I choose to play dumb for now.

Celia shakes her head at me and replies simply, "Derrick who else could it be?"

I let a little laugh out and say, "Well I'm sure his wife's cakes can be classified as poisonous at times, but...?"

Shone laughs, "Oh, please! No, it is much more serious than that -apparently.." she pauses for effect ".. now don't quote me but I overheard that this is something to do with the girl who committed suicide."

My face has a blank look. Both Shone and Celia shake their heads dramatically.

Celia says, "Don't you ever watch the news for goodness sake child! My god, your Nana would have been all over this. That young girl who jumped of Markhall Bridge a few days ago. Apparently Derrick pushed her!" She pauses and opens her eyes wider at me for effect and then grabs herself the nearest chair to her and sits down shaking her head. "I am so glad his poor mother is not alive to see this. Oh, the poor soul, may she rest in peace."

Shone comes closer to me but stops when she sees my slight flinch. She says in a very soft voice, " I … I don't know if your Nana ever told you about Abi, I mean your mum, and Markhall Bridge …"

Celia gasps, "Oh God, how could we all be so silly and forget – oh god!" She moves up quickly and offers me her seat like I might faint. she herself now has tears brimming in her eyes.

I shake my head at the offer of the seat, and I do my best to offer them my sad smile. I nod slowly.

"Yes, Nana did tell me, but it never made any sense to me. I never knew her and … well I don't know … I can't dwell on it to be honest and Markhall Bridge is famous for this sort of thing really." I reply quoting a tweet I had read earlier. "They really should do something about that bridge."

"Oh god, but I don't understand," says Celia. "The police are over there now, you know, they have taped off his house, his office , they have sealed his car. Poor Maryanne, she's packed off back to her mum and dad's with the kids and the dog." She sighs for a quick breath and shakes her head. "I mean what is going on, and why would he push a young girl off a bridge?"

I just stand there and shrug my shoulders. "I'm going to get myself some tea – would you like anything?"

Celia and Shone both say, "No thank you."

Shone adds, "Let me get it for you."

She checks my preferences and goes off to get me my tea, making sure she stops to talk to as many people as she possibly can on the way to the tea stand. I hear the words "Abigail", "Markhall", "Derrick" and "mum" being muttered not so subtly. It spreads through the tea room like wildfire in the dry Australian bush. I feel their eyes on me like a million ants crawling on my skin, but I stand tall and try not to give in to the feeling of chucking up on all of them.

"So Derrick, huh?" I say. "I wonder why the house is all taped off. Have you had a chance to go and try to talk to one of the officers? I'm sure they would talk to you – I mean you do run most of the community support programs around here and surely everyone in Valhan needs to know if they are safe or not?"

Celia is nodding incessantly as I speak. "Yes, yes, oh dear god, you are right. I must go and find out." She pauses for a sip of water and then carries on. "I mean what if he is let back out , we must know if we are safe , he could be like one of those crazy people on the American shows you know; Murderer in my village. What if he tries to murder a young girl in our town? Oh god, I must go there at once and find out!"

She almost springboards up from the chair like an athelete as I offer to walk with her, but she waves me off and marches on with a certain stride and a look that is quite forceful. For such a sweet lady, Celia looks

peculiarly like some warrior about to take on the

biggest dragon she has ever seen.

Shone comes back with my tea. I smile politely and take the cup from her, shuddering as her hand brushes mine. The tea is lukewarm. I won't be drinking that ;not even to keep up appearances. Tea has got to be the right colour and warmth for its medicinal effects to work, and for me lukewarm and a tad too milky is not medicinal, it's torture. Shone smiles, oblivious to my ordeal, and carries on like one of the most affluent people in your community getting arrested is normal.

"So where has my mum gone off in such a determined state?"

"Oh, I'm not sure. I think she mentioned something about getting some more info from the officers outside Osborne's house." I laugh casually. "I think she is going to interrogate the police at the house or the office , it will

depend on which route she chooses I suppose ..."

Shone groans. "Oh God, what is up with my mum? Seriously, she has already tried getting information from one of the officers, but they just brushed her off."

"I am curious," I said. "What makes you think Derrick pushed this girl off a bridge? What's the story?"

"Well! Basically some kid jumped off this bridge the day before yesterday and everyone just thinks it was some random suicide, but last night the police come rushing into Valhan at full speed. I was just sitting there and next thing I see these blue lights flashing past my window."

A small fact for you: Shone lives two doors down and around the corner from Derrick.

"Well of course I grabbed my jacket and shouted to Rich that I was just popping out to see what had happened." Shone stops and looks around to see who else is listening and she isn't disappointed. There are plenty of greedy ears nearby and faces who offer better reactions than mine. So she carries on dramatically, her voice slightly louder and her arms waving a bit more than normal. "Well of course by the time I got around the corner, all I saw was Derrick being bundled into the car. I tried to speak to his Mrs, but she's a funny one at the best of times!" This statement generates a lot of agreement, with nods and verbal "*yeahs*". "I mean she just stood there, but I am sure I heard one of the police officers say that it was great work that they had caught the man responsible for that girl's death."

I hear the tuts and the gasps around me as everyone takes in what has been said.

"Who would have thought it,' said Shone. "We have a child murderer in our little Town; Derrick Osborne. I mean he always was a bit weird, but this is just ugh!" She shudders and some nearby lady comes over and gives her a hug whilst they both talk about how this affects them so much.

I nod and I slowly make my excuses and leave. I try not to act too excited. I stay quiet. I hear the murmuring whispers behind my back about how brave I am and how I have managed so well since Nana died. They all think I am a tragic survivor, just like my Nana was. I like that they believe what I wish them to believe.

Once I leave the hall, I straighten my back, smile and walk purposefully toward Derrick's house. Like the many others who have come to see what's going on, I slow my pace. The adrenaline rushes through me, but I keep calm and look concerned and as I go past his house. I see Celia giving some poor officer all her what fors as she struggles to gain any information.

I walk over to Celia and calmly smile at the officer, who looks relieved that I am about to take this pestering old busybody away from him. I smile politely at Celia and say, "C'mon, this officer is just doing his job. He wouldn't be very good at his job if he gave you details." As my heart thumps loudly, I smile at the officer sympathetically and he returns my smile with a nod. I calmly reply, "Please do let me know if I can be of any assistance, we are a small community and would love to be of any help."

The officer replies with a soft curtness, "That's very kind of you and I am sure if we need your help we will be asking for it."

I nod and usher Celia away before she can start another rant on how she could single-handedly solve everything if they would just let her know what was going on. As I walk away, the officer smiles at me and whispers a silent, "Thank you." I in return give him a single nod of my head and direct Celia to a crowd of Valhanians who are greedy for any new snippet of information.

I double back, round past Shone's house and toward the high street, and I see the barricaded offices of Derrick Osbourne. Here, quite a few nosy people have gathered around as if they might see the police bring out a score of dead bodies, but sadly they will be disappointed as the only thing that will be leaving here will be computers, files and phones.

As soon as I come back to my sanctuary, I head up and cleanse myself from the impurities that have been spoiling my skin. Once I feel thoroughly clean, I come downstairs and make myself a good strong cup of tea. I sip it slowly as I look out into the garden. It's a graveyard to most flowering plants right now, trees with no leaves and scores of twiggy shrubs, but I know soon enough the plants and the flowers will begin to flourish. For now I enjoy the barrenness of it all and I walk to the back of the garden to sit in the gazebo and fully appreciate the silence.

I head back into my study and log straight back into the Baileys' cameras. Sitting on the couch is Chloe and another friend called Amy. They both are huddled together and just nodding. Chloe is talking to Jamie.

"I am not sure. She seemed so quiet the last few weeks. I mean

I just thought she was angry at me because I had hooked up with Oliver's friend."

"Did Oliver ever harass her or anything," asks Jamie. "Is there anything at all you can tell us?"

"No, no," says Chloe. "Oliver has been busy. I mean at the start he was always asking Emma for more, but she always said no, and he was good about it. But he is always playing his stupid computer game. He's also been hanging about with some new girl who is a friend of his sister."

"Oh God," Jamie starts to cry slowly. "Chloe, I don't know … I was hoping you could tell us something. The Police will want to talk to you at some point you know?"

"My mum said they might, and I understand," says Chloe sadly.

Natalie comes into the room with Mathew who is intrigued by the new faces in the room.

Chloe walks over to Mathew and tries to pick him up to hug him, but Mathew looks at her and decides he doesn't want to be picked up by her. He clings closely to Natalie.

"Oh ignore him," Natalie says, "he's been a bit whiny today."

"Emma was always sending pictures of him to us …" Chloe replies and starts to cry.

Amy gets up. They both make excuses about getting back home and they both walk out of the room looking sad.

Natalie sees them out and then walks back over. She puts Mathew down and puts on the My First Teddy app on the iPad. Mathew is happy watching his favourite teddy on the screen.

Natalie goes over to Jamie and they both hug and cry, clinging onto each other for support.

Emma's mum hasn't gotten out of bed and dad has been lying next to her for support. They both are silent. No ifs, buts, what ifs – all just a deep and suffocating silence.

For now I push the Bailey household to the back burner and read up on the messages from Emma's friends.

In the BFF's WhatsApp group Chloe had started the conversation first.

CHLOE
OMG OMG have you heard about Emma … {Crying face emoji}

AMY
{Crying face emoji}

Followed by lots more crying and sad emojis from all their friends.
Mostly the conversation is between Chloe, Amy and Hazel.

CHLOE
I threw up when I found out oh god. {pic of tear stained face, sick emoji}

AMY
I just can't stop crying I am not sure what happened – I tried asking her over a few weeks ago but she said she had work to do.

HAZEL
Yeh she said no to me too – I asked her why she had gone so quiet but she had just said she was busy with school assignments.

CHLOE
I don't know. I think we should go over and speak to her parents.

HAZEL
I can't it is too awkward.

AMY
I will come but we will come back out soon.

CHLOE
I will ask my mum. I just feel so sad {sad face emoji}

I feel terrible. I feel like we hardly spoke the last few months. I really wish we could have spoken – I don't know what to do, I am going to speak to my mum – I just feel so sad.

AMY
I will come over I feel the same too.

I switch off for now and carry on with my work.

# CHAPTER SIXTEEN

Emma's mum has hardly spoken in the last couple of days. She has had many breakdowns and although she had tried her best to vent at the procedures that followed her daughter's death she eventfully gave in and had to be given more medication to help her with her increasing panic attacks.

The coroner's inquest had to be carried out, even though there was enough evidence to suggest suicide without foul play – Emma's scrunched up suicidal post-its, the depressing and sad notes saved into her computer. It was part of the formal process and had to be done.

All the unused pills and empty bottles were collected from where Emma had hidden them, but as time had lapsed Emma had become less methodical in trying to hide the empty bottles and pills. Of course George was always there to distract her when it had looked like she was about to throw them out.

Her toxicology reports showed that she had seven times the amount of recommended alcohol limit in her body. Although the bereavement officers had tried their best to use all their tact, compassion and professionalism, Emma's parents had both erupted like volcanoes, spilling their anger onto anyone who could hear.

"Don't you think I would know if my daughter was an alcoholic or a junkie," screamed Emma's mum.

"Are you sure? I mean it just doesn't sound like our Em. I think you have your reports muddled – this is not who our daughter was," added Emma's dad simply.

He said it with controlled anger and frustration, but also with a certainty that would have the best of experts second-guessing their own work. He even went to find her school reports to show the officers: like the reports were a gilded charter of who his daughter truly was.

In this instance, the officer was trained to a high standard and repeated the facts again – simply and directly. To show some level of compassion she added, "It's hard to believe it of your own children I understand that, but sadly these results are from Emma's samples."

Now in Emma's living room, Jamie, Natalie, and Emma's mum and dad sit face to face with the leading detective team tasked with finding out what had happened. Mathew sleeps in the bedroom upstairs whilst the family keep a watch on him via his video baby monitor.

Both of Emma's parents are sitting in the same spot they had sat in when Emma had come into the room a couple of days ago – when she had stood so silently.

Detective Gill and team has been put in charge of Emma's case. They are a motivated team of high performing and high achieving officers, and firmly believe that this is why they have been able to finish up this case so quickly and so efficiently. What these fools don't know is that my meticulous planning, doggedness and sheer will is the reason why Emma's case has come together so easily. However, I don't need the glory of this – my story is different.

There is an awkward shuffling. Detective Gill is keen to share the outcome of the case but has come with the bereavement officer so that she is reminded not to be too excited whilst talking about what she and her team have discovered. In truth it's mostly down to her newest recruit, Paul, who is a "computer genius".

My take on his genius is that he is actually very able and competent with his skills. I wouldn't quite rank him up to my levels but I must admit when I was watching him work systematically through the evidence I had cleverly left for him, he was curious, and at times shrewd.

His desire to go running back to his seniors with his findings was almost subdued. He would second guess his own work and meticulously check and cross check everything before he presented his findings. These kind of skills impress me a lot. However, like I have said, I would call him competent but not a genius.

Officer Gill is an elegant, tall lady. She is in her 30s and has her vibrant reddish hair neatly pinned back. Although on first appearance she looks soft and vulnerable with her big blue eyes and delicate features, her demeanour shows that she is no pushover. She is now looking over at the bereavement officer. They silently communicate and Officer Gill softly clears her throat before she starts.

"I am going to start by apologising for a few things," she says in a fairly firm voice. "I know the tabloids have gone crazy and I know you have felt we have not communicated our findings with you clearly, but I must be clear that until we had the absolute truth we couldn't confirm anything. Sadly, as you may know, the Press does like to pick hot topics and make them into something they are not."

She waits for the reactions from the four very different people sat around her – she barely gets a response from three, but Emma's mum is quick and sharp with her response and this makes the bereavement officer sit on edge just in case Emma's mum lashes out.

"I really don't give a shit about your stupid apologies or what the stupid press has to say – I just want to know why my beautiful … aaahhhh … oohhh." Emma's mum starts to shake, sob and groan at the same time. She hits the side of the sofa with her curled hands and Emma's dad is quick to be there beside her and holds her. She leans into him and wails.

"Shh, honey, we need to hear this. We need to know," he says.

They hold onto each other as they cry and slowly their sobbing subdues into incoherent mumbling. Emma's dad looks over at the officer and gives her a small nod.

He holds onto his wife. They both look like they haven't had a shower for weeks, their skins pale with greasy hair sitting almost like seaweed on their heads – I can almost smell their foul stale human stench from through the cameras. I shiver at the thought.

Officer Gill says, "I guess it is best we all sit down and do this. I have chosen to come here and speak with you, not that it's going to make it easier, but at least you can relax – in the offices it would be harder." She looks over at Emma's mum and glances over to Natalie and Jamie. "I think perhaps it would be wise to get some tea or water just," she nods over at Emma's mum discretely, "to help everyone get back together. It is important that we are all ready, emotionally and physically."

Emma's mum pipes up quickly, "No no. I don't need anything – I just need to understand … I have to … I can't stop thinking about what she was going through and how this has all happened …"

She starts sobbing again into Emma's dad's arm. Natalie gets up and asks who would like what to drink and walks off toward the kitchen. Jamie kneels down beside his mum and subconsciously pats her knees whilst leaning into his parents.

Mathew is still asleep and for a moment all is silent.

Jamie cautiously asks, "This has been very hard – I mean it's hard for anyone to lose some one, but like this?" He pauses and looks up at his parents. He gets up and takes a deep breath. "Officer Gill, I really hope you can just help us clear up all this mess and is there any way to stop the stupid media – we are too scared to turn on the TV or go outside. It's making it all a lot worse."

Jamie pauses in the middle of the room, as he struggles with whatever he is thinking he must say.

"Well the media should stop now because now anything they say or publish can jeopardise the case. After today they can't publish any more. We sadly do not have control over what people type in social media."

Jamie rubs his face with his hands. "How can so many people comment so callously about our family – some of these people are suggesting we are some sort of murderous, chavvy, incestuous types ..." He can't finish his sentence and he walks over to the baby camera monitor and looks at Mathew sleeping. He smiles, but it's loaded with sadness. I can see the sadness reflected in his eyes also. Natalie comes in with a tray full of tea and biscuits. Jamie walks over to her and takes it from her and offers it around the room. Both of them keeping themselves sane by being busy, by having some form of routine. I have noticed how both have filled their day with meaningless and endless tasks to keep themselves busy and when they have nothing to do, they use Mathew as a comforting toy. It's almost like he is their security blanket.

"I think it is best if you don't read the speculations by the masses on the internet – people write what they think without realising the impacts of their words. It's almost like they forget that the person reading their comments is human."

"We just need some answers." Jamie sits down and it's almost like it is a signal for them to start hearing about what the police force has been doing to find out why they lost Emma. "I believe you have someone under arrest?"

At this point the whole family look at Officer Gill with such intent that it feels like she can bring Emma back with a wave of her baton. Although she has been in some rough situations in her lifetime, Officer Gill finds herself almost choking, but she brings in her years of training. Sticking to the facts, she pulls herself together and begins.

"Yes, you are right, we do have someone one under arrest. We believe ..." At this point she pauses and takes a deep breath, then continues with what she knows will be hard to digest, even harder than the death of their daughter. "We believe your daughter was in touch with and groomed by a man called Derrick Osborne – is he someone that you know ... Derrick Osbourne?" She says the name much slower the second time around.

All four look at each other with blank faces and almost unanimously shake their heads.

"Derrick was chatting to Emma under a false name. He was pretending to be the same age as her. Did Emma ever mention a boy named George? George Elliot?"

Once again blank looks all around and this time Emma's dad says, "No, but surely if she was involved with anyone we would know. We were close. She barely went out and spent most of her days studying. Those names don't mean anything to us. Why would this man be chatting to her with a different name ... wait did you say pretending to be the same age, and groomed? How much older is this bastard? Emma isn't that stupid ... shit ... shit."

"Get out of here!" Emma's mum is on her feet and pointing an accusing finger at Officer Gill. "Just get out – who the hell do you think you are coming in here and telling me all this bullshit about Emma, this is all fake..."

The support officer gets up and calmly and professionally ushers Emma's mum out of the room.

"I think it is best to carry on without her being in here if that's OK?" No one responds, so the silence is taken as agreement. "So in answer to your question, Derrick Osbourne is in his early fifties. On the face of it he is a respectable and trusted member of his community. Our investigations, however, have shown him to be interested in girls around Emma's age. We found some sites that he was interested in showing girls in their mid-teens." What she fails to mention to the Bailey family is that by some sites she means the porn stream. That I had sent toward Derrick's computer had all been of girls who were around 15. What you people don't understand is that just because it's on some porn site doesn't mean it's legal. There are lots of sites where younger people are used with or without consent and in most countries this is illegal but it's rarely monitored online.

"We believe Derrick contacted Emma casually through a Twitter stream and they became close after that."

The rest of the Baileys sit in silence, all looking horrified and sick. As Officer Gill had predicted this part may be harder to deal with: even more so than Emma's suicide.

"From what we see looking through his computer and Emma's, he started off with a friendship under the alias of George and slowly started to isolate her. He is the reason why Emma started drinking and taking pills: he has taken advantage of a stressful time in Emma's life. He saw her fragile state, where she was feeling lonely and suicidal and exploited it. We believe that on the night Emma died, she was supposed to be meeting him. We are all still unsure of what happened, but we believe that Emma may have panicked when she realised that George wasn't who she thought he was and we believe she jumped to get away from him."

"I don't understand – she knows about internet safety – she was almost like the school champion for online safety and stranger danger online." Emma's dad almost gets up again as if to find another certificate, but he sits down.

"We have sightings of Derrick's car in the vicinity and footage of where he was seen near Emma's school."

This time Natalie speaks – she is the quieter one in their family, but even now she is struggling to make sense of everything.

"Can you tell us what he is saying? Does he even have any remorse for what he has done? You are saying there are some parts of the story that you are unsure about – why is that? What is his account of all this and what were his plans had Emma got into his car? Was he planning on abducting her? She may have fallen for him online, but Emma would never have gone quietly – she is – or was such a smart kid." Natalie has tears on her face as she asks the million questions, but she is curious and she gets nods of agreement from Jamie and dad as she asks her questions.

Gill clears her throat again and begins the tale of Derrick and how he groomed their daughter online. Mentally ticking off each question in her head as she speaks.

Slowly each person in Emma's family falls silent and lets Gill speak. Then in their daze they let Gill and her colleagues leave, and they all sit silently wondering how their poor child had fallen into such a horrible trap.

Jamie and Natalie carry on making the funeral arrangements.

His parents sit there looking at the screens around them, but they don't take anything in.

# CHAPTER 17

*I feel awful. I don't know what to do. I told mum last night about the pregnancy. She didn't take it well. She kept reminding me of the myth that our family home was built on the bones of those who sinned. Mum's ancestors had come from the very first Vicar's family and my dad's from the person who had braved all odds to create this haven. Growing up we were all told that our town was protected because it was built on the blood of sinners and no sin could pass its boundaries. What a load of old-fashioned nonsense!*

*She must have repeated that story a thousand times! I am sitting in my room and I have nothing to do. Mum said I should give the baby up for adoption. I don't know what to do. I still haven't heard from David.*

A broken heart and a sad face are drawn next to her messy handwriting. The page looks like it had once been wet – the diary had soaked up her tears and left a crumpled page as evidence.

#

Now that the heat has died down since Derrick's arrest and Emma is fast becoming another statistic, I start to log back into the Bailey household. Jamie and Natalie have sort of moved in for as long as they feel his parents need them. They had been renting their place so this made sense. It has added to Jamie's commute, but not much more than fifteen minutes. Mathew is loving the attention from his grandparents and fast becoming the life and soul of this household. This very quiet household.

Emma's mum sits on her usual spot, her iPad now back in her hand. She has put earphones on as she doesn't want to watch the show Jamie and Natalie are watching, but she doesn't want to sit alone either. She can go days without crying and then suddenly she will not stop crying. Her dad  on the other hand didn't mourn for too long,  it didnt take him long to connect back with his Skype chat he has been handling the death differently. I have noticed that he has been drinking a lot more than before. He dismisses any help from Jamie and has told him to leave him alone.

Jamie and Natalie have been discussing his dad's behaviour a lot and once again as he excuses himself, Jamie cautiously looks over at his mum and watches her engrossed in the iPad.

"He's gone off again, Nat."

"Babe, you've tried talking to him. We can't keep pampering him – he just doesn't want to talk about it."

Jamie looks at the empty space left by his dad

"I found some more empty spirit bottles. I spoke to him about it and he just shrugged it off. Told me to mind my own damn business. I even spoke to the doc about it but it seems until he helps himself no one can help him." He sighs and finishes with, "He always has been difficult. We've never been able to talk about stuff like this."

Jamie leans into Natalie and gives her a huge cuddle. She leans into him and they both settle into a content place as they watch some new all singing and dancing  warlords tv show. Both Natalie and Jamie have struggled with their loss of Emma, but both have been incredibly practical and supportive of each other. They have almost dealt with her death in a very practical way. Little Mathew has helped them find that happiness at this time. I watch them all – each one of them gearing themselves up for the big day tomorrow. Most of the arrangements have been done by Natalie with guidance from Jamie and sometimes some input from Emma's mum. Nobody ever talks about Emma's funeral and if they do it is in a formal and informative manner, and as the evening draws to a close, one by one they all finish up their tasks and head off for bed – to face one of the hardest days since Emma's death.

The day didn't brighten up just because it was Emma's funeral. Wouldn't that have just been ideal. Another useless chitchat item people talk about. What the fucking weather was like on the day of someone's funeral. I swear scientists didn't ever need to invent the anaesthetic – some of these dull conversations you humans have would have that desired effect.

I gear myself up to attend her funeral. The funeral was open to everyone and from looking at the numbers attending, it was going to be a big one. I would blend in quite easily. I had gone down to the village hall and that stupid Shone had said she might go, but I casually put it out to her that someone going from the same town as Derrick may be a tad insensitive. That had washed away any desires she had to attend. She was only going so she could come back and be the queen bee for a day or so till the next dramatic turn of events took away everyone's attention from the deeds of Derrick.

I was looking forward to seeing the Baileys in real life – the excitement bubbled away inside me and I was surprised at this, surprised that it generated such a feeling. I don't think I have ever been this enthusiastic about anything.

The dress code was strictly no black; the funeral was to celebrate Emma, not to mourn her.

From my limited access to their house, I got snippets of information. Jamie had physically thrown up when he had seen Derrick's picture. Again, lots of silence. They had all seemed relieved to find out that the pervert had not been able to molest, rape or prostitute her out to paedophile gangs.

The media around Emma's death has been subdued mostly to prevent any miscarriage of justice. The Twitter trends have stopped completely – Emma's death has now become yesterday's news for those outraged keyboard warriors. There are just a few handfuls of people that are still suffering with the loss.

I choose dark, but not black, clothes. A hoodie, a cap and tinted glasses. Of course I don't need glasses, but I am using them to blend in. I can't risk being caught, but I have to attend and keep the probabilities of being caught very low. I have chosen my route where there are no CCTV spots. My journey there and back will be an invisible one.

I had done it once before. I had gone to the Bailey house and sat outside for some hours one day, hoping to catch a glimpse of them all. Especially her dad.

I have arrived early and there are already people here. I can tell they are here for Emma as they are all dressed similar to me but in less dark clothes. I mull around some people just listening to what everyone has to say. Then I go into the toilets and find an empty cubicle to change my attire.

I lurk around the darker, shadowy areas. It's easy enough to do and anyone who had the time to watch me would just think I was trying to keep away from the spitting rain. The great thing for me is that even at a funeral parlour you stupid humans have got your eyes glued to some technology. That works for me. Less people to look at me. Once, before this new age disease of technology hit you humans, when I walked out, I would get people looking at me. I am attractive and I have this aura of self-confidence. Both men and women would flock toward me hoping to know me. In Valhan, locals learnt quickly of my cold behaviour and I was often mocked for thinking too much of myself. Since Nana's death most now try being nice. Not because of how I look – it is for my money – they respect and tolerate me because of my wealth.

The small courtyard part of the funeral parlour is filling up fast. I feel claustrophobic with all these smelly humans around me. Occasionally, the other guests' eyes linger on me, but I keep my head straight and try not to focus on anything. I have managed to find a spot near the front where the cars will come. My skin is tingling from the excitement of seeing them all.

Slowly the hearse pulls up. I can see Chloe and company all huddled right at the front of the crowd and just as the hearse is about to stop the crying and sniffling noise levels go up. People have started to cry – some sobbing, some gulping for air. There are a lot of tears.

I am not focused on any of them – I look beyond the hearse

and see the customary family car pull up behind. The hearse almost creates a blind spot. I try and look through the flower arrangements to catch a glimpse of them all. My heart thunders at the thought of soon being so close to them. I am sure my pupils have dilated completely.

Jamie is the first to get out – he has Mathew already in his arms – followed by Natalie and then dad.

Both Natalie and dad reach forward to help Emma's mum out of the car. She is the only one dressed in black – black jeans and a black t-shirt with a rainbow, one of Emma's favourites. Her mum wears it under an open black cardigan. Emma's mum is still struggling. She has sunglasses on, even though it is dull and slightly raining.

I feed off her misery. It makes me insanely happy. I keep a straight face. I am almost too scared to blink in case I miss something.

As the coffin is taken in, the  sobbing and crying gets louder. Inside, soft background music is playing – some Ariana Grande tune. I am not listening. I follow in the middle of the crowd. I am sitting two rows behind the Baileys – I had to use my elbows to push some sobbing old granny out the way to get my position – my eyes locked on the people at the front. I can't let them get out of sight, not even for a minute.

I look at the shapes of their heads – how they each respond to their grief. Jamie and Natalie pass Mathew between them.

Now the service starts. Jamie gets up and starts the process. He talks of his annoying sister, his partner in crime – the duo who fought with each other, but also of how they had stuck together when they were plotting against their parents. He tells those listening of her little quirks, like how she would always get up early on Christmas morning and hide his presents, so that she could open hers first. Then his shoulders heave up and down. He shakes his head and allows the tears to flow as he mumbles ever so softly, "Goodbye Sis, sleep well." He knocks gently on her coffin as he walks past.

I watch. I have no tears, no emotions. I hear everyone around me starting to sob and howl at their loss, the front row all struggling to breathe – I can see the rise and fall of their backs.

Emma's dad gets up next – he is still working the comatose look. He looks at the crowd and says very simply, "We lost our Emma because of a monster – who is now behind bars. I strongly urge you all to be aware of who you talk to online." He looks directly at the group of kids that are all huddled together at the back. "Please learn from what happened to our girl. Don't ever let that happen to you." He walks off. His message sobers everyone up quickly.

They have gone for a cremation service rather than a burial. Instead of holding the wake they have decided to send the money to a charity that supports people from online bullying and grooming.

At the end of the service, the Baileys all stand at the side of the doorway so that people can pay their respects as they pass by.

I walk slowly, shuffling in the line, my senses in full alert as I come closer, and I can almost hear the conversation in my head. I have never been nervous about anything … I don't suppose I am nervous now – more exhilarated. A bit like a lion stalking a deer is the best way to describe it. My heart is pumping blood around my body at full pace and it is helping me stay sharp. Keeping me focused.

I am positioned well. In front of me I have some kids from Emma's class, and behind me people who are relatives. Only about 20 people ahead of me now – I can start to hear conversations again. People paying their respects – " Sorry for your loss", "My thoughts and prayers will be with you", " Please call us if you need support" – all condolences and messages of support, and the Baileys all just stand there nodding and trying to make polite conversation.

Mathew has been passed to Natalie's parents and he is in the background adding his two bits worth of babble to the conversations, bringing smiles to some of the surrounding sad faces.

My body is fully tense now as I walk along. I feel like a sniper would in the desert marking his shot – picking his enemy and just waiting for the right moment.

I hold back a little to let the crowd of kids go through. They just mumble stuff about how much they will miss Emma and how she was the best.

Now it is my turn. Jamie, Natalie, Emma's mum and then Dad.

I slowly remove my glasses and walk toward Jamie. I look him in the eyes. He is a couple of inches taller than me and I hear the soft sharp breath as he looks at me. Oddly, I look more like him than Emma did.

I pass my condolences to my half-brother, who was 11 months old when I was born. David, our father, had been cheating on his wife when she had just given birth to their first born Jamie. There is exactly 337 days between our birthdays. I smile sadly. Perhaps it is a genuine smile of sadness as out of this whole family, he is the one I relate to the most, the one I feel most connected to. But I keep my distance – I cannot allow useless humans emotions ruin what I have. I use his confusion as he tries to work out why he thinks he recognises me.

"I am sorry for your loss, Jamie. Emma was like a sister to me."

Jamie nods, but can't get rid of the look confusion on his face. He turns his head vaguely to the next lot of mourners as I walk on and allow the people behind me to get to him.

I ignore Natalie and Emma's mum and move directly towards her dad. And now, finally, I am face to face with the man who I had never thought I would meet. I take deep breath. David Harvey Bailey: my father.

He looks up. Confusion crosses his face as it had done with Jamie. He raises an eyebrow as if hoping I will answer the , "Who are you again?" question that he is too polite to ask. I break my own rules of human touch, lean forward and clasp both his hands in mine. His hands are cold. Maybe the effects of a panic attack or high anxiety. I want to say so much more but I cannot right now. I see him looking at me, the battle of recognition and confusion in his eyes as clear as daylight.

I look into his eyes – a mirror of my own.

*The baby looks like you, the same beautiful brown eyes and brown hair.*

The words from Abigail's letter echo through my memory.

"I am sorry for your loss,' I say. "Emma was like a sister to me."

I see the confusion grow in his eyes. As he blinks, some remaining tears slide slowly down his face. My eyes break contact to watch the trail, but I can't stay longer, for if I do – all will be lost. This man is the reason I have suffered so much and now I will ensure he suffers the consequences of his actions. Emma was the first step.

I purposely look deeply into his eyes again – I see the confusion, the questioned recognition, more confusion and at that point I decide to move on forward into the bustle of mourners. I release his hands, for now, from my iron grip.

I feel his eyes on my back. The softness of his skin still lingers on mine – it's not disgusting to me like it normally would be, but I know it will irritate me soon enough. I hold my head high and walk away slowly. I put on my glasses and walk away from David Harvey Bailey.

\#

The letters that had arrived on the day of Nana's cremation had served one purpose and that was to give me a location. It isn't too hard to find a David, second name unknown, if you have a rough location. Most people don't move too far from where they grow up – especially around these parts.

It didn't take me long – working out from Abigail's diaries and those letters what age my dad would be. A simple census search showed that the town had a population of 8,346, but take in some of the neighbouring areas and you are looking at a grand population of 26, 720. Then take in that fifty two percent of this population were female. Just under ten percent were a David, and the majority of them David Smith. Once I filtered for age, I was left with four Davids that were eligible.

Abigail had used more primitive methods like the Yellow Pages and had found what would have felt like a million Davids – it is a top-ranking name year on year after all. From her letters it was clear she was already in a mental state of no return. For me it was easier – my method was meticulous. It hadn't taken me long to find him and from there, to find Emma. I smile as I walk away slowly from the funeral. A feeling of enlightenment puts an extra menace in my prowl.

#

As I come back into Valhan, I see that the hall is buzzing with people, and although I want to go home and shower, then spend a day alone away from people, curiosity gets the better of me. I pull over and walk toward the hall.

Celia jumps in front of me within minutes, her face free of her usual lipstick and mascara – she looks visibly shaken.

"He's killed himself – the guilt must have been too much – today was the funeral and he's killed himself!"

"Who has? David…?" Shit, I've said that without thinking … shit, shit, shit … train your mind and speak with your mind not your emotions. Shit. "Celia!" I grab her shoulders to steady both of us, breaking the no human touch rule twice in one day. "Who are you talking about?"

"Derrick … who else? They found him dead in his cell. Oh, he's killed himself!" Now she starts crying. "You know I was hoping he wasn't guilty – in my heart somewhere I was hoping he wasn't guilty." She sobs. "Did you know he fought with his parents when we all learnt about Abigail being pregnant with you. His dad came over to talk to my Harry about it. He told him that Derrick said he loved Abigail and wanted to take care of her. His dad wouldn't have it. He was old-fashioned and they had a huge row about it. We all knew Abigail hated the attention Derrick gave her, but Derrick was besotted by her. Maybe that is just who he was – a person who liked to hound young girls …" Celia pulls out a family heirloom type handkerchief from her mini-suitcase-style handbag and dabs her eyes with it. "I hope this is the end of all of the horrid things happening in Valhan. It's been a horrid time – I'm worried about the younger kids here. Life just used to be simple when we were younger."

With that, Celia turns her back and walks back into the hall. She is consoled by the locals who have shown up. Derrick, whatever he was, was liked by plenty of people. The son of one of the original founding families, some of his ancestors stand with mine in many of the old photos in the hall. There is genuine shock and sadness as people carry on talking about the events that led to this day.

I am not sure how long I stand there or even how I get myself home. Although Derrick wanting to take care of Abigail seems noble enough, I think of his children, the pampered prissies, and I'm glad that this never happened to me. I would rather take a hundred beatings from Nana every day than have had him as a father.

I am showered now and back in my space in the attic. I have taken off the dress my mother had worn, the one I had salvaged from her room, I wonder if he ever thinks of her and his child he conceived, did he remember the dress that she had worn that day, that carefully chosen dress. Today there is no music. Today, I just lie here and allow myself to enjoy the feeling of floating in space. I haven't even switched the planetarium lights on. I just lie in the dark. My thoughts consume every living cell in my brain. That battle he had going on his eyes, I had wanted to reach out and touch his face, I had wanted to tell him, slap him but I had kept my cool, I had worn that dress as a shield to remind and protect me of how callously he had turned his back on Abigail, and me: Isobel Amber Godfrey. I Am God and for now, I lie in the darkness ridding myself of the silly emotions, they escape my body in the form of tears and as they leave so do any questions of my father. Today I feel I have righted the wrongs of my father. I lie here floating in an eternal darkness at peace with my past.

Today, Imogen Amber Godfrey will sleep a good night's sleep. I Am God.

Printed in Great Britain
by Amazon

82213768R00098